MODERN
NATIONS
—OF THE—
WORLD

INDONESIA

MODERN
NATIONS
—OF THE—
WORLD

INDONESIA

BY DEBRA A. MILLER

LUCENT BOOKS

An imprint of Thomson Gale, a part of The Thomson Corporation

Detroit • New York • San Francisco • San Diego • New Haven, Conn. • Waterville, Maine • London • Munich

THOMSON
★
GALE

On cover: Jakarta, the capital city of Indonesia

LIBRARY OF CONGRESS CATALOGING-IN-PUBLICATION DATA

Miller, Debra A.
 Indonesia / by Debra A. Miller.
    p. cm. — (Modern nations of the world)
 Includes bibliographical references and index.
 ISBN 1-59018-442-4 (hard cover : alk. paper)
 1. Indonesia—Juvenile literature. I. Title. II. Series.
DS615.M48 2005
959.8—dc22

2005005738

Printed in the United States of America

CONTENTS

INTRODUCTION

A DANGEROUS PARADISE

Indonesia, a tropical country in Southeast Asia, is made up of thousands of beautiful islands. Many of the country's islands are home to natural wonders, such as rich rain forests, exotic wildlife, towering volcanoes, pristine beaches, and brilliantly colored coral seas. The numerous, often isolated islands also have produced a multitude of fascinating cultures, which have contributed to a rich and thriving arts scene, a wealth of local handicrafts, and many different and delicious cuisines. The Indonesian islands are truly one of the world's most remarkable and magnificent spots—in many ways a paradise on earth.

Not surprisingly, parts of Indonesia were discovered long ago by American and other tourists. The island of Bali, in particular, has gained a reputation as a wondrous destination for Western tourists. As travel writer Bill Dalton explains, "This beautiful isle . . . exactly fits the Western definition of a tropical paradise, famous for its charming people, lovely scenery, and the sophisticated artistry of its distinctly Indonesian-Hindu civilization."[1] In fact, Bali for years has attracted as many as a million visitors annually.

This seemingly wonderful paradise, however, is often spoiled by very earthly dangers and problems. Most think of Indonesia today, for example, as the site of one of the world's most deadly disasters—the December 26, 2004 tsunami—which left hundreds of thousands of Indonesians and foreign visitors dead, missing, injured, orphaned, or homeless. The tsunami was caused by an earthquake on the ocean's floor that created huge waves that, crashing with great fury on the coasts of northern Indonesia, wiped out whole villages. Although other world disasters in the past have killed more people, the tsunami received an unprecedented amount of TV and press coverage, partly because many of the victims were tourists from around the world. Tsunamis are only some of the island chain's natural dangers, however. Located in an active seismic zone that stretches across the equator, Indonesia is also prone to land-based earthquakes, volcanic eruptions, and flooding caused by heavy rainstorms called monsoons.

Human activities, too, have helped make Indonesia a dangerous place. For centuries the region's many resources have attracted explorers and traders from both far and near. Migrants from Indochina and China were some of the first inhabitants, followed by Indian and Arab traders, and later, Europeans who colonized the region for hundreds of years. The result of these many influences is not only a highly diverse culture, but also deep social and religious divides that have long plagued the country.

As the world's largest Muslim country, for example, Indonesia has recently been experiencing the effects of Islamic extremism. Although Indonesia traditionally has been known as a very moderate Islamic country, several extremist Islamic groups have formed in Indonesia to promote a more rigid Islamic society, through both violence and political action. This trend has resulted not only in episodes of Islamic terrorism, including a much-publicized 2002 bombing of a Bali tourist spot, but also in violent Muslim attacks on Christian churches and villages and a political push for more restrictive, Islam-based laws.

An Indonesian woman performs a traditional dance on the island of Bali. The many islands that comprise the nation of Indonesia have produced a multitude of vibrant cultures.

Some parts of Indonesia also have sought to break away from the country to form their own independent nations, creating ongoing separatist violence that has pitted government troops against rebel fighters on several of the country's islands. One of these areas, East Timor, was finally granted its independence in 2002 after many years of Indonesian military repression and reports of atrocities committed by Indonesia's army. Two other areas, however, remain hot spots—the northern part of the island of Sumatra, called Aceh, and the region of Irian Jaya, often called Papua. In both areas, rebels are still fighting battles with the Indonesian army, seeking full independence from Indonesia. The side effects of such violence have been thousands of civilian deaths and the destruction of many people's homes and farms.

Economically, too, Indonesia has faced challenges. First arriving in the late sixteenth century, the Dutch colonized the islands as part of the Dutch East Indies Empire. For more than 350 years, the Dutch exploited the islands and forced many peasants to work for meager or no wages. By the time the Dutch withdrew and the nation of Indonesia was born in 1949, poverty was an entrenched problem. In subsequent years, Indonesia managed to modernize its economy and reduce the levels of poverty, but a financial crisis in Asia in 1997 virtually destroyed these gains. The nation is only now recovering.

Moreover, Indonesia has only recently achieved a democratic form of government, after decades of authoritarian, military rule that made the country a dangerous and difficult place to live. From the time it achieved independence from the Dutch in 1949 until the 1990s, the country was ruled by only two presidents—Achmed Soekarno and General Soeharto—whose regimes were run largely as dictatorships that became known for their corruption, military repression, and human rights abuses. In 1998, Indonesians finally rejected this type of government and turned to democratic elections. Recent leaders have finally begun the process of changing Indonesia by embracing a freer press, curbing the power of the military, and cleaning up government corruption. Much, however, remains to be done. In 2004, Indonesia elected Susilo Bambang Yudhoyono as president, and he now shoulders the challenge of molding Indonesia's future. With good leadership, perhaps one day the region's islands will transform into a safer, more peaceful, and more prosperous place—a true paradise in every sense.

A NATION OF ISLANDS

The country of Indonesia is a vast archipelago, or group of islands, located in Southeast Asia. This string of islands, often called the Malay Archipelago, comprises more than 13,677 islands surrounded by the Pacific and Indian oceans and the South China Sea. In fact, Indonesia is the world's largest island grouping, stretching across three time zones and extending for 1,100 miles (1,760km) from north to south and for 3,200 miles (5,120km) from west to east. Added together, the many islands create a huge country covering 741,096 square miles (1,926,849 sq. km), or an area about three times the size of Texas. Located on the equator, the islands have the benefit of a warm, tropical climate, which together with their varied geography, creates an incredibly rich and diverse environment. As travel writer Peter Turner describes, Indonesia's islands are like a "string of jewels . . . [spreading] from the Asian mainland into the Pacific Ocean."[2]

INDONESIA'S MAIN ISLANDS AND ISLAND GROUPS

Indonesia is made up of some of the largest islands in the world. In fact, just five large island territories represent close to nine-tenths of the nation's land. These five large island regions, in descending order of size, are Kalimantan, Sumatra, Irian Jaya, Sulawesi, and Java. Kalimantan, part of the world's third largest island, is almost the size of Texas. Sumatra and Irian Jaya are also quite large—each roughly the size of California. Sulawesi is about the size of Washington State. Java, although the most populated island, is relatively small—only about one-third the size of Japan. Four of these islands—Kalimantan, Sumatra, Sulawesi, and Java—are known as the Greater Sunda Islands because they all lie on the Sunda Shelf, a shallow, underwater extension of the Asian mainland. Irian Jaya, on the other hand, lies far to the east in another shallow ocean area called the Sahul Shelf.

In addition to the five main islands, there are two major island groups within the Indonesian archipelago—Nusa

SOUTHEASTERN ASIA

Tenggara and the Maluku Islands—and as many as sixty smaller island groupings. Nusa Tenggara, also known as the Lesser Sunda Islands, stretches eastward from Java toward Irian Jaya and is made up of hundreds of islands. The area is dominated by several relatively large islands—two main islands in the west, Lombok and Sumbawa, and three main islands in the east, Flores, Sumba, and Timor. The eastern part of the island of Timor voted in 1999 to form an independent country called East Timor, but the western part of the island still belongs to Indonesia. The Maluku Islands, the second of Indonesia's major island groupings, lie in the northeastern part of the nation's territory, between Sulawesi and Irian Jaya. The largest islands in this archipelago are Halmahera, Seram, and Buru. These are the famous "Spice Islands," renowned during earlier centuries for their production of rare spices, such as cloves, pepper, and nutmeg.

Two of Indonesia's island territories are shared with other nations. The nations of Malaysia and Brunei share Kalimantan (formerly called Borneo); Irian Jaya shares New Guinea, the world's second largest island, with the nation of Papua New Guinea. Other countries that lie near Indonesia include Thailand, Cambodia, and Vietnam to the northwest, the Philippines to the northeast, and the island nation of Australia to the southeast.

BALI: A TOURIST'S HAVEN

The tiny island of Bali, situated just south of the much larger and heavily populated island of Java, is Indonesia's most popular tourist spot. In fact, nearly half the hotels in all of Indonesia are located on Bali, and the island long has welcomed more than a million visitors per year. Bali's popularity is not hard to understand. Known as the Hawaii of the East, it has a tropical climate, sandy white beaches, lush rain forests, beautiful scenery, and an astounding variety of plants and animals. The Balinese, in particular, love flowers, which they often use in their Hindu religious ceremonies. In fact, many of the flowering plants that westerners cultivate as potted plants, such as poinsettias, coleus, and begonias, grow wild in Bali's tropical climate. The people of Bali also have helped to make the island a magnet for tourists. The Balinese are known to be friendly, open, and eager to share their arts and culture. Today, however, mass tourism has clearly taken its toll, and Bali is increasingly becoming overpopulated, overdeveloped, and environmentally stressed. This decline, and recent terrorist attacks, such as the 2002 bombing of a Bali nightclub, have begun to reduce Bali's tourist numbers.

A tiny tropical paradise, the island of Bali has long been the prime destination for tourists visiting Indonesia.

Bali, one of the most famous and popular of Indonesia's islands among westerners, is actually a tiny island that is home to less than 2 percent of the nation's total population. Located just east of the much larger island of Java and next to Lombok, Bali is only about the size of Delaware, but is notable for its great beauty and variety of landscapes. Here tourists find everything from sandy beaches to alpine highlands and monsoon-fed rain forests.

MOUNTAINS AND VOLCANOES

Most of the Indonesian islands are very mountainous. Rugged mountains can be found on larger islands, such as Sumatra, Java, Bali, Lombok, Sulawesi, Seram, as well as on the smaller island chains of Nusa Tenggara and Maluku. The Maluku Islands, for example, rise very steeply out of the deep sea, creating very few level coastal plains. Irian Jaya, in particular, is known for its spectacular, tall mountains. In fact, some parts of the Jayawijaya Mountains and the Sudirman Mountains in Irian Jaya are so high that they remain snow-capped year-round. The island's highest peak, Puncak Jaya, for example, towers 16,532 feet (5,038.9m) above sea level.

One of the most striking features of Indonesia's mountainous areas is their many volcanoes. A line of more than four

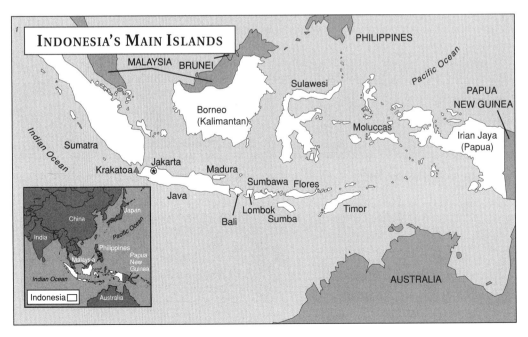

THE KRAKATOA EXPLOSION

Even before the 2004 tsunami, Indonesia was famous as the site of a massive geological event felt around the world—the 1883 volcanic eruption on Krakatoa island off southern Sumatra. Krakatoa exploded with the force of more than ten thousand times that of the atom bomb dropped on Hiroshima at the end of World War II. Quite literally, it was the loudest sound ever recorded. In an instant, two-thirds of the island disappeared into the sea, and all life on the island was completely obliterated. The volcanic eruption also generated a huge, seven-story-high tsunami that hit Indonesia's

shoreline in Sumatra and Java, wiping out 160 villages and killing as many as forty thousand people. Smaller tsunamis were detected as far away as the English Channel, Alaska, and South Africa. The tons of ash that were thrown into the air affected global weather for many years and led to spectacular sunsets that were painted by famous American and European artists of that era. News of Krakatoa, like news of the 2004 disaster, was relayed around the world. Although telephones and televisions had not yet been invented, the wireless telegraph made the event almost instantly a global news story.

In this 1995 photo, smoke billows from the Krakatoa volcano, which erupted with explosive force in 1883.

hundred great volcanoes, a formation called the "Ring of Fire," stretches southward along the western coast of Sumatra and then runs west to east through Java, Bali, and Nusa Tenggara. Volcanoes can also be found in the Maluku Islands and in northeastern Sulawesi. About one hundred of these volcanoes are currently active, and the entire region, especially Java, is subject to frequent volcanic eruptions. Between 1972 and 1991 alone, some twenty-nine volcanic eruptions were recorded, mostly on Java. Other islands have not been exempt from volcano damage, however. In 1963, for example, Bali was rocked by an eruption of the Gunung Agung volcano.

Indeed, various parts of Indonesia have been the site of some of the most violent volcanic eruptions in recorded history. In 1815, for example, a large eruption on the north coast of Sumbawa in Nusa Tenggara killed more than ninety-two thousand people. Ash from the eruption darkened the skies around the world and, as reporter Dan Murphy explains, caused the following year, 1816, to become known in places such as the United States and Britain as "the year without a summer."[3] One of Indonesia's most violent eruptions, however, occurred decades later in 1883 when a volcano on Krakatoa, an island between Java and Sumatra, erupted. The massive explosion destroyed two-thirds of the island and killed more than thirty-six thousand people. Krakatoa's volcano then fell silent until the late 1970s, when it erupted twice more.

Because of the rugged and mountainous topography, much of Indonesia remains undeveloped. In fact, only about 10 percent of the nation's island land is suitable for farmland. Much of the richest farmland is on Java and Bali, where the islands' many volcanoes have produced deep layers of volcanic soil filled with nutrients and minerals.

RAIN FORESTS AND SWAMPS

Largely because major parts of Indonesia's mountainous terrain have not been developed for agriculture, the country has kept a rich and diverse environment marked by significant rain forest reserves. Although heavily logged, Indonesia's forests still cover more than half of the country and represent almost 10 percent of the world's remaining tropical rain forests. Only Brazil, the home of dense Amazon rain forests, has more tropical forest land than Indonesia. In fact, because of the size of its rain forests, as freelance writer Peter Halesworth notes, Indonesia has been dubbed "the Amazon of Southeast Asia."[4] Most of these forests are found on Sumatra, Kalimantan, Sulawesi, and Irian Jaya. Java, too, at one time was covered in rain forests, but these disappeared centuries ago when its land was cleared for agriculture.

Unfortunately, Indonesia's remaining rain forest areas today are disappearing due mostly to unregulated logging of their valuable hardwood trees. International experts estimate, for example, that each year more than 3 million acres of the country's tropical rain forests are destroyed. Moreover, the rate of deforestation is increasing, and some species of hardwood trees have been logged so heavily that they have nearly disappeared from the islands. Still other areas of forest are lost to poor farmers using so-called "slash and burn" agricultural methods, in which sections of rain forest are cleared by burning them and then farmed until the nutrients in the soil are gone. At that point, the farmers simply move on to other areas of forest, where they begin this process again. So far, the Indonesian government's efforts to slow deforestation have been weak, largely because timber revenue is so important to the nation's economy.

The lush swamps found along the low-lying shores of many of its islands are another important feature of Indonesia's environment. Along the east coast of Sumatra, the south coast of Kalimantan, Irian Jaya, and much of the northern coast of Java, for example, the land is broken by numerous

More than half of Indonesia is covered with rain forests, which are shrinking at an alarming rate due to unregulated logging activities.

swampy wetlands anchored by unique tropical trees, called mangroves, that grow with their roots in the water. These swampy areas are an important part of the nation's tropical ecosystem. Formed at the mouth of rivers, the mangrove swamps help to control erosion of riverbanks and provide a barrier between the land and the ocean that helps protect against storms and high winds. The groves also create a rich habitat for a wide variety of marine creatures, including fishes, crabs, and shrimp.

Like the rain forests, however, Indonesia's mangrove swamps are being lost to development. Many are being converted to create ponds for the commercial production of fish and shrimp. Estimates suggest that Indonesia's mangrove swamps, which only decades ago occupied close to 8 million acres, now take up less than 6 million acres.

DIVERSITY OF FLORA AND FAUNA

Indonesia's still-rich environments encourage an astonishing diversity of flora and fauna. Indonesia's tropical forests, for example, are so biologically diverse that they are considered to be one of the richest depositories of genetic material in the world. Here, experts have found over 40,000 plant species, about 5,000 tree species, 1,500 bird species, almost 500 species of mammals, 7,000 species of fish, and 1,000 species of reptiles and amphibians. In fact, although the country occupies only 1.3 percent of the earth's land surface, it provides habitat for 10 percent of the world's plant species, 12 percent of the mammal species, 16 percent of the reptile and amphibian species, and 17 percent of the bird species.

The country's natural environment, however, is divided into two completely different ecological zones—a western zone and an eastern zone. These zones were first identified in the mid-1800s by British naturalist Alfred Wallace in his classic study, *The Malay Archipelago*. Since then, the dividing line between these two environments has become known as the "Wallace Line." This line runs along the edge of the Sunda Shelf between Kalimantan and Sulawesi, then southward between Bali and Lombok.

The lush western zone sports some spectacular flora, including the world's largest flower, the rafflesia, which creates a bloom as large as 3 feet (0.91m) across. The western zone is also home to large land animals, such as elephants, tigers,

In addition to orangutans, the western zone of Indonesia is home to such large mammals as elephants and tigers.

and leopards, as well as ocean creatures, such as sea turtles. In addition, one of the western zone's most well-known native animals is the orangutan (meaning "person of the forest"), a unique type of long-haired red ape found only on Sumatra and Kalimantan. This beast can grow as large as a man and lives in the forest canopy, where it travels by swinging from tree to tree.

The drier eastern zone has a climate more like that of Australia. Irian Jaya is home to many types of Australian marsupials and reptiles. These include not only kangaroos, but also marsupial mice, possums, crocodiles, and frilled lizards. Also in this zone are islands that have developed highly unique species. The island of Sulawesi, for example, is known for its *anoa*, or dwarf buffalo, which stands only about 31 inches

(78.7cm) tall; the *babi rusa,* or deer pig, which sports huge tusks from the side of its mouth; and the beaked hornbill, a spectacular bird species. The Maluku Islands, on the other hand, are noted mainly for their butterflies and bird life, particularly the brightly colored *nuri raja,* or king parrot. In addition, the Komodo dragon, the world's largest lizard, is found only in the islands of Nusa Tenggara.

THE KOMODO DRAGON

Indonesia is the only place in the world one can find Komodo dragons—the world's largest lizards. The dragons live on the hot, dry, volcanic islands of Komodo, Rinca, Flores, and several other small islands in the East Nusa Tenggara island group. Most of these islands are now part of Komodo National Park, a protected habitat for the creatures. The Komodo dragons can grow to 10 feet (3.05m) in length and weigh as much as 200 pounds (91.72kg). They drool constantly, have long, forked tongues, and a keen sense of smell. Most of the time, the dragons move around slowly on large, stout legs. However, they are ferocious predators that can move as fast as a dog and kill their prey with strong, powerful jaws. In fact, they typically kill and eat large creatures such as goats and deer. They are also capable of killing humans, and many stories are told in Indonesia about dragons eating people. Even if they are not able to kill their victims on the spot, the saliva they deposit in their attack is so full of bacteria that, if untreated, their bites quickly become infected and eventually result in death.

A pair of Komodo dragons mates during breeding season. Komodo dragons are found on several Indonesian islands and nowhere else in the world.

The loss of habitat from deforestation, however, has destroyed many of Indonesia's wildlife species. Indonesia's list of endangered species now includes about 126 birds, 63 mammals, and 21 reptiles. Elephants, once very numerous, can only occasionally be found living in the wild on Sumatra and Kalimantan. Tigers and leopards, which once roamed throughout Asia, now exist only in parts of Sumatra. All of these animals, however, as well as other even more endangered species, such as the one-horned Javan rhinoceros, can be seen in special nature parks, such as Kalimantan's Tanjung Putting National Park and Java's Ujung Kulon National Park.

A Tropical Climate

Indonesia's great biodiversity is made possible largely by its tropical climate. Indonesia is situated on the equator and is surrounded by warm ocean waters, conditions that give it uniform temperatures and humidity year-round. Temperatures average about 88°F (31.11°C) in coastal regions, but much cooler temperatures prevail farther inland and at higher elevations. Snowy, winter conditions can even occur at some of the country's highest elevations. Humidity is typically quite high, ranging between 70 and 90 percent.

The biggest weather variable is rainfall. There are two seasons, the wet season (October to April) and the dry season (May to September). During the wet season, Indonesia can receive significant amounts of rain, as much as 78 inches (198.12cm) per year. Rain often comes in the form of monsoons, hurricane-like storms caused by wind currents from Mainland Asia and the Pacific Ocean. These storms blow through the region during the monsoon season, which is usually between December and March. Rainfall in Indonesia varies, however, from island to island. Western Sumatra, Java, Bali, the interior of Kalimantan, Sulawesi, and Irian Jaya receive the most rain, while islands closer to Australia, such as Nusa Tenggara, tend to be much drier, often receiving less than 39 inches (99.06cm) of rain per year. Other islands, such as the Maluku Islands, receive varying and unpredictable amounts of rain, depending on the direction and strength of local winds.

Indonesia's climate and geography, unfortunately, also make it subject to some of nature's most destructive forces. The monsoons often cause flooding of farmlands and villages.

In addition, not only are earthquakes and volcanic activity quite common, but they often cause tsunamis, which in an island environment can cause extensive destruction. This great danger was most recently demonstrated in December 2004, when a historic and massive tsunami hit the Indonesian region, destroying entire villages and leaving as many as 243,530 Indonesians dead or missing.

NATURAL RESOURCES

Along with periodic danger, however, the country's climate and geology also give Indonesia many natural resources. For a long time, Java's rich, volcanic soils have made it the center of the country's agricultural industry. Rice, the staple food of Southeast Asia, has been grown in flooded fields on Java for more than two thousand years. The island also traditionally produced commercial crops of coffee, sugarcane, cocoa, rubber, tea, and spices. Today, some traditional crops are still grown, including rice, cloves (a popular Indonesian spice), and sugarcane, but newer crops, such as corn, have also been added.

Indonesia's forests, too, have long been a great resource for the country. Wood has historically been used as an energy source for homes, and in recent years the exporting of many of the rich hardwoods of the rain forests has produced revenues that have helped the country's economy to grow.

In addition to rich soils and forests, Indonesia is also blessed with mineral resources and plenty of oil and gas. Oil and natural gas fields are found in and off the shores of Java, with major fields located in Aceh and East Kalimantan. Current known reserves will be depleted within about a decade, but experts are hopeful that new deposits will soon be found. These outer islands also produce metals, such as tin, copper, and nickel, while Java has deposits of phosphates and manganese. The nation is just beginning to explore other, renewable energy sources, such as solar, water, and geothermal energy. All of these new energy sources have great potential given Indonesia's equatorial location, mountainous terrain and rainfall, and many volcanic areas.

Finally, Indonesia is rich in ocean resources. Although the fishing industry is not as large as one might expect, given the vast stretches of shoreline, many small-time fishermen still make their living from the sea. Experts say this fishing and shrimp industry has room for expansion.

SETTLEMENT PATTERNS, POPULATION, AND CITIES

Indonesia's diverse geography and environment have led to various types of human settlements. Altogether, approximately six thousand of the islands in the Indonesia archipelago are inhabited. Many Indonesian peasants live in the valleys and plains of Sumatra, Java, and Bali and grow rice for a living. In the largely Islamic coastal communities, the people are typically engaged in fishing, business activities, and trade. Still other Indonesians live in the interior mountain forests, where they survive through subsistence agriculture. Because of the country's lack of development funds, however, few modern cities exist and many Indonesians still live in small, rural villages.

Despite Indonesia's lack of urban development, however, its population numbers more than 238 million, making it the world's fourth most populous nation, after China, India, and the United States. The most densely populated island is Java, where more than 128 million people live in very crowded conditions. Many Indonesians also live on Sumatra and the other larger islands.

A fisherman in Banda Aceh sorts through the day's catch. Indonesia's waters are extremely rich in ocean resources.

The growing population has forced Indonesia's farmers onto smaller and smaller plots of land, and this in turn has caused many peasants to leave their native areas to search elsewhere for new opportunities. Many of Java's residents, in particular, have fled its severely overpopulated center. Some migrated to rural areas on other islands, but many of these displaced Indonesians have moved into the country's few urban areas, creating growing problems of urban poverty, pollution, and crime.

Indonesia's three major urban centers are Jakarta, Surabaya, and Medan. Jakarta, the nation's capital, is located on Java and is home to more than 9 million people, making it one of the largest cities in the world. It was founded by the Dutch, who called it Batavia. Little of the European legacy remains, however, and much of the city today is made up of poverty-stricken slums. Yet Jakarta is also the political heart of the country and a major industrial center and seaport. The city's main attractions are the Merdeka Monument, a monument to the country's independence, the old city (called Kota), the Great Mosque of Istiqlal, and several museums, including the impressive National Museum. In addition, Jakarta boasts more than one hundred schools of higher learning, including the University of Indonesia, the country's oldest university.

Surabaya, the second largest city in Indonesia, with a population of more than 2 million, is also located on the island of Java. It is a major seaport and one of the main industrial and trading areas of the country. Exports such as sugar, tobacco, coffee, corn, and tapioca are brought by railway to its port from throughout Java and shipped around the world. Medan is a slightly smaller city on the island of Sumatra. Like Surabaya, Medan is a trade center for the interior of its respective island for agricultural and forest products.

Although much of Indonesia remains a tropical paradise, the country and its natural environment are clearly becoming more urbanized. This urbanization is forcing the people and their government to contend with overcrowding, resource exploitation, and pollution problems that are common to many developing nations.

A Dutch Colony

Indonesia's beauty, location, and rich resources have for centuries attracted different foreign peoples. Early visitors included Indian, Chinese, and Arab traders, who brought their unique cultures and religions to the islands. Later, Dutch explorers colonized and exploited the region for its spices and other products for hundreds of years until independence was finally achieved in 1949.

Earliest Inhabitants

The earliest inhabitants of the Indonesian archipelago are believed to have come from India or Burma as early as five hundred thousand years ago. Evidence of these early human ancestors was found in 1891 by archeologists working in Java. These archeologists uncovered fossil remains that they called *Pithecanthropus erectus*, or "Java Man." Experts say Java Man and his descendants lived in small hunting and gathering groups and eventually began using simple tools. Java Man either became extinct at some point or mixed with other peoples who later migrated to the region.

Many of these later migrants to the Indonesian islands came from southern China and Indochina around 3000 B.C. These people were called Malays, and by about the seventh century B.C., they had established organized societies in the Indonesian archipelago. They lived in small villages, where they grew rice in carefully irrigated fields, domesticated farm animals, made pottery, worked with copper and bronze, and learned seafaring skills. Like many other early peoples, their belief systems were animist; that is, they believed that all objects in nature were inhabited by spirits and that these spirits could be influenced by offerings, rites, and ceremonies.

Eventually, the small villages banded together and evolved into small kingdoms that were ruled by local chieftains. These cultures flourished along the coasts and increasingly began to make contact with traders from other parts of Southeast Asia.

EARLY HINDU AND BUDDHIST KINGDOMS

Some of the earliest foreign traders to arrive on the shores of the Indonesian islands were from India. Indonesia was located on the sea-lanes between India and China that were used by early Asian traders, and by the first century A.D., this crossroads position made the area an established trading center for India. The relationship with India allowed the island peoples to trade local items, including rare spices and herbs that grew on the Maluku Islands (as previously noted, the "Spice Islands"). At the same time, Indian traders brought Indian culture to Indonesia. Some of the most significant of India's imports were the Sanskrit language and the Hindu and Buddhist religions. Chinese traders also came to Indonesia, but their influence was less significant than that of India's traders.

By the end of the seventh century A.D., an India-influenced kingdom called Srivijaya had developed along the coasts of eastern Sumatra. The people of Srivijaya followed the Buddhist religion, and the kingdom became a strong sea power that controlled the region's trade. These trade activities brought Srivijaya great wealth until sometime in the twelfth century, when the kingdom's power began to decline.

During this period, other civilizations were developing in the inland parts of Java. In the early eighth century, for example, a Hindu civilization, called the Mataram kingdom, arose in eastern Java. The Mataram people later became part of the Buddhist Sailendra kingdom, which arose in central Java between the eighth and tenth centuries. The Sailendra were great builders and today are known for building a huge Buddhist temple complex called Borobudur, which contains many low-relief stone sculptures that illustrate Buddhist religious principles. This kingdom was the beginning of modern Javanese culture.

The last great Hindu kingdom to develop in Indonesia was the Majapahit, which was founded in eastern Java in the thirteenth century. The Majapahits established a broad empire that encompassed many of the islands of Indonesia. As historian Datus C. Smith notes, "This Majapahit Empire . . . was probably the biggest Indonesian nation until the birth of the Republic six and a half centuries later."[5] The Majapahit Empire remained strong until the death of its most prominent ruler, Hayam Wuruk, in 1389. Thereafter, the kingdom's

power ebbed, especially after it faced rising trade competition from growing Islamic kingdoms in the area.

Javanese rulers of the Sailendra kingdom began building the massive complex of Buddhist temples called Borobudur more than twelve hundred years ago.

THE COMING OF ISLAM

Islam, a religion that was established by the Prophet Muhammad in the Arabian Peninsula in the seventh century, first began spreading into the Indonesian archipelago as early as the eleventh century. Muslim inscriptions found in Java date to this period. Over many centuries, numerous Arab traders traveled to the Indonesian islands and slowly converted indigenous people to their faith. By the thirteenth century, many people in Sumatra had converted. By the fifteenth and sixteenth centuries, even Indonesian rulers began turning to Islam, and they made it a state religion in many regions of Indonesia that once had been controlled by the Majapahit Empire.

By the end of the sixteenth century, the time of the first European trading explorations in the area, there were two main Indonesian kingdoms—the Melaka kingdom in Java and the Makassar kingdom in southwestern Saluwesi—and both were Muslim. Founded in 1400 by a descendant of the rulers of Srivijaya, the Melaka kingdom developed as a rich trading empire and completely controlled trade in the archipelago throughout the fifteenth century. These robust trading activities helped to spread Islam farther throughout the surrounding islands. The Makassar kingdom in Sulawesi developed a bit later, at the end of the sixteenth century, and grew to prominence as a sea power whose sailors traveled as far as Australia.

However, Islam, like earlier religions embraced by the peoples of Indonesia, was often modified to include native Indonesian beliefs. Many Indonesians, for example, converted to Islam but also continued to believe in certain animist, Hindu, or Buddhist ideas or practices. This was particularly true in interior areas of central and eastern Java, which, as history professor Robert Crib explains, "became dominated

Young Muslim girls inside a mosque in Banda Aceh study the Koran. Centuries ago, Arab traders introduced Islam to the islands of Indonesia.

by an Islam [that] had intimately blended Islamic doctrine with Hindu and animist elements to create a distinctive belief system called *Kejawen* [also called *Kebatinan*]."[6]

EUROPEAN COMPETITION FOR INDONESIA'S SPICE TRADE

The first Europeans to visit Indonesia were the Portuguese. In the late 1400s, Portuguese explorers set out to seize the rich Asian trade routes and gain control over the trade of nutmeg, mace, and cloves from the Spice Islands. At the time, these spices were much sought-after by Europeans, making them highly valuable commodities. The Portuguese presence in Indonesia, however, was limited both in size and resources. As a result, Portugal's hold on the region was soon challenged by other European powers, including Spain, Britain, and the Netherlands, and a trade war ensued in the Indonesian archipelago.

It was the Dutch who finally managed to control the islands of Indonesia, oust competing powers, and exploit the region's rich spice trade. The first Dutch expedition, led by Cornelius de Houtman, arrived in Indonesia in 1596 and returned to the Netherlands with a cargo of valuable spices. Other expeditions soon followed, as did the building of the first Dutch fort—dubbed Batavia—in western Java. Soon, several Dutch merchant companies banded together to form the Dutch East India Company, which operated under the control of the Dutch government.

Although it was a business enterprise, the Dutch East India Company was given broad authority by the Dutch government to make treaties and wage war, as well as conduct trading activities. Using these broad powers, the Dutch East India Company soon took control of Java, kept other traders out of the region, and dominated the Indonesian spice trade. When other countries' trading companies managed to penetrate the Dutch defenses to trade for some spice products from outlying islands, the Dutch brutally killed the Indonesians involved in the deals. The Dutch East India Company therefore rapidly progressed from being a mere trading company to being enforcers of a valuable Dutch trading monopoly in Indonesia.

By the middle of the eighteenth century, however, the Dutch East India Company's power began to deteriorate. Instability resulting from various revolts and wars among

Java's indigenous kingdoms forced the company to spend increasing amounts of its resources on armies and security. Also, other countries began growing spices in other parts of the world, reducing the Dutch East India Company's monopoly. In 1799, the trading company was terminated, its possessions were turned over to the Dutch government, and Indonesia officially became a Dutch colony. The town that had grown up around the fort at Batavia became its colonial capital.

THE DUTCH COLONIAL EMPIRE

For the next 350 years, the Dutch ruled Indonesia as a colonial power and exploited not only its spice trade but also much of its other resources and wealth. Colonial policies were inherently unfair and exploitive, benefiting only the Dutch rulers while leaving most of the Indonesian population impoverished and virtually enslaved. For much of this period, however, Dutch control was not complete. Many islands, including Sumatra, Bali, Lombok, and Borneo (today called Kalimantan), remained largely independent, and fighting often flared up between Dutch troops and local populations.

The most significant Indonesian resistance to Dutch rule occurred from 1825 to 1830, a period that became known as the Java War. The war began when the Dutch decided to build a road across a property owned by Pangeran Diponegoro, the eldest son of a local Javan aristocrat. The property contained a sacred tomb, and the sacrilege inspired Diponegoro to lead a revolt against the Dutch. Joined by both Indonesian elites and peasants, Diponegoro waged a five-year guerrilla war against Dutch troops, until the Dutch ultimately arrested Diponegoro and suppressed the uprising. By the end of the war, however, more than two hundred thousand Javanese out of a total population of only 3 million had lost their lives.

Following their victory, the Dutch reinforced their control over Indonesia through a form of indirect rule in which Dutch overseers governed at the top but implemented their decisions through a local administration made up of aristocrats descended from ancient Javanese rulers. With this cooperation from local Indonesian leaders, the Dutch were able to exploit the peasantry and reap rewards from their la-

The Early Spice Trade

Early in Indonesia's history, ports on Java and Sumatra became centers for the trading of goods between the East and the West. At these ports, traders from India, Arab countries, and European countries bought produce from China as well as locally produced items from Indonesia's islands. Some of the most important local trade products were the spices produced on the Maluku Islands, called the "Spice Islands." Europeans, especially, craved the wonderful tastes and properties of spices such as pepper, cloves, and nutmeg, as well as rare herbs and scented woods and oils. Cloves and nutmeg, for example, were not only valued by the Europeans as a food seasoning; they also were used as food preservatives, breath fresheners, and as a medicine for the relief of colic, gout, and rheumatism. The great demand caused the prices of these spices to soar, and at the time, the Malukus were the only known source. It was this excitement over the spice trade that first brought European traders to the Indonesian region, and it became the motivation for the establishment of the Dutch East Indies colonial empire.

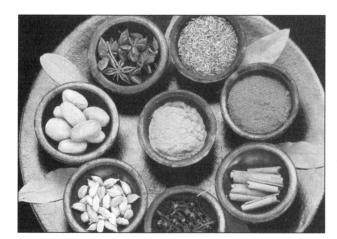

An array of typical Indonesian spices is shown here, including nutmeg, cumin, cinnamon, and cloves.

bor. This system was called the Cultivation System because it established a government monopoly over various agricultural products and required each village to grow export crops—such as coffee, sugar, indigo, tea, cinnamon, pepper, tobacco, cotton, and silk—to be sold to the Dutch government at set prices. The Dutch then traded these products on the world market and made large profits. For Indonesian peasants, however, this system paid very little and prevented them from growing rice and other food crops. Corruption

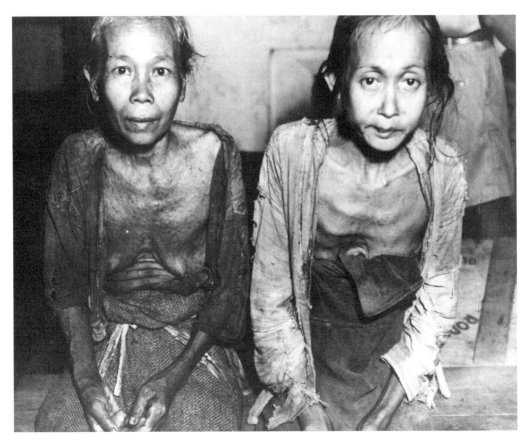

Under the Dutch government's Cultivation System, most Indonesian peasants like these women were abused and forced into destitution.

and abuse were also rampant. As a result, the majority of Indonesian peasants sank further and further into poverty, illiteracy, and famine. By the end of the nineteenth century, the entire archipelago labored under the Cultivation System and tight Dutch control.

Despite the terrible treatment of the local population, however, Dutch domination imposed a political unity on the region that, for the first time in history, organized the many separate Indonesian islands together as one nation. As social scientist Donald M. Seekins explains, "The modern state of Indonesia is in a real sense a nineteenth-century creation. It was during this century that most of its boundaries were defined and a process of . . . political, military, and economic integration was begun."[7]

Furthermore, during the latter period of colonial rule, widespread Indonesian poverty and increasing opposition to colonial policies by the Dutch public prompted the Dutch government to adopt a more compassionate approach toward the island populations. The government-controlled Cultivation System was dismantled in favor of a private system that allowed goods to be sold at market prices. New products, such as rubber and oil, were introduced during this period, and economic prosperity improved the lives of both European residents and local Indonesians.

In 1901, the government also introduced the Ethical Policy, a social reform plan under which the Dutch built schools, improved health care, and tried to encourage many people from overpopulated Java to move to other, less populated islands. By 1940, eighteen thousand village schools were constructed that provided a Dutch education to at least forty-five thousand Indonesian students. In addition, medical and technical schools were established to train doctors and medical workers, and expenditures on public health were increased dramatically. Politically, however, the Dutch retained control over Indonesia.

Indonesian Nationalism

Ironically, the education programs begun by the Dutch introduced the Indonesian people to Western ideas of freedom and self-determination that would eventually lead to Indonesia's independence from the Netherlands. In 1908, for example, a group of students from a school for doctors in Java formed the first political association that advocated Indonesian independence. It was followed by other independence movements, including Saredat Islam, a movement sponsored by Muslim organizations dedicated to Islamic rule. The strongest early pro-independence group to emerge, however, was the Indonesian Communist Party (PKI). Established in 1920, the PKI quickly became popular among trade unionists and rural Indonesians. It led several insurrections against colonial rule in western Java and Sumatra, but the government put down the rebellions with force and jailed PKI leaders.

The spread of Indonesian nationalism, however, could not be stopped. The people by this time had tired of a system that diverted Indonesia's wealth into profits for foreigners and allowed them virtually no voice in their own affairs. Stepping into the void created by PKI's disappearance was a new organization, the Partai Nasional Indonesia (PNI), which continued to

challenge Dutch rule and proved to be Indonesia's most significant nationalist group. The PNI was founded in 1928 by
Achmed Soekarno, a European-educated Muslim who advocated a secular Indonesian government and attracted a large
following among the Indonesian masses. Soekarno, however, also had rivals. One of these was Mohammad Hatta,
who founded a competing organization called Indonesian
National Education, or the New PNI.

As demands for independence grew, the Dutch authori-
ties soon recognized the threat posed by Soekarno and Hatta
to their rule. Both were arrested; Soekarno was even imprisoned and later exiled to a distant island. In Soekarno's absence, the PNI fell apart and was replaced by another
independence party, the Indonesia Party (called Partindo).
Without strong leadership, though, Partindo was easily suppressed by the Dutch.

WORLD WAR II AND JAPANESE CONTROL

During World War II, Japan's invasion of the Dutch territories in the Pacific crippled Dutch power in the region. When
Japan occupied the Indonesian islands in 1942, the Dutch
Indonesian government surrendered, offering no resistance, and the Japanese promptly took control. The Japanese changed Batavia's name to Jakarta, arrested and
imprisoned all Europeans, and imposed their own system of
government.

The Indonesians greeted the Japanese as their liberators,
and their expulsion of the Dutch became a turning point in
Indonesian history. As social scientist Seekins explains, "The
Japanese occupation . . . shattered the myth of Dutch supe-
riority, as Batavia gave up its empire without a fight."[8] The
Japanese also allowed Indonesians to participate more in
their own government than did the Dutch. Although Japanese military officers occupied the highest government positions, Indonesians were placed in many lower positions
previously held by Dutch officials. The Japanese even encouraged and cooperated with Indonesian independence
leaders, such as Soekarno (who returned from exile) and
Hatta, both of whom the Japanese respected for their ability
to influence large numbers of Indonesians.

The Japanese, however, quickly revealed themselves as
brutal masters. They were interested in Indonesia only for its

A SPEECH BY PRESIDENT SOEKARNO

Achmed Soekarno was the leader of Indonesia's independence movement and became the country's first president in 1949. Throughout his political career, Soekarno was a fiery and effective speaker. Excerpted here are parts of a speech Soekarno gave on December 19, 1961, urging Indonesians to support one of his major foreign policy initiatives—the military annexation of Irian Jaya:

> At this present moment, the Dutch are setting up a puppet state in West Irian, partitioning it from the Republic of Indonesia . . . establishing a "state of Papua.". . . What should the Republic of Indonesia do? . . . Oh, yes, in the UN [United Nations] we can execute diplomacy, in the UN we can fence with words, we can use this argument and that argument in the UN, this reason and that reason . . . [but] it is already clear there are no results. . . . There is nothing else to do, we here must act. . . . And that is why I now give a command to the entire Indonesian people. . . . Defeat this "state of Papua"!

The speech excerpts are taken from Papua Web, an online resource.

In 1952 Indonesian president Achmed Soekarno tries to appease an angry crowd calling for immediate popular elections.

resources and large population, both of which could be used to aid the Japanese war effort. In addition to forcing local peasants to work on economic and wartime defense projects, the Japanese, with the help of independence leaders, organized thousands of Indonesians into a volunteer Indonesian

army, which was expected to fight an expected Allied invasion. By the end of World War II, close to sixty thousand Indonesians had been mobilized into the first Indonesian army.

In late 1944, as the tide turned against the Japanese in the
war, the Japanese promised to grant Indonesia independence, hoping this gesture would inspire Indonesian loyalty
and support. A group of Indonesians, called the Preparatory
Committee for Indonesian Independence (PPKI), was organized to draft a constitution. In what became known as the
Jakarta Charter, the PPKI recognized Islamic law but decided
that Indonesia should not be an Islamic state. PPKI chose
Soekarno as president and Hatta as vice president. Soekarno,
in a speech in 1945, set forth the philosophical principles

*A mushroom cloud
rises in the sky after an
atomic bomb is
dropped on Hiroshima
in 1945. The terms of
surrender after World
War II forced Japan out
of Indonesia.*

around which the new nation of Indonesia would be united. These principles, called *Pancasila* (a Sanskrit word meaning "five principles"), included: belief in one God, humanitarianism, Indonesian unity, democracy by consensus, and social justice for all Indonesians. Before independence could be officially declared, however, the Allies dropped atomic bombs on Japan. On August 15, 1945, the Japanese abruptly surrendered, ending World War II.

Immediately following the end of the war, Soekarno was pressured, primarily by young soldiers in the newly formed Indonesian army, to proclaim Indonesia's independence. The situation was chaotic, however, because although the Japanese had surrendered, no Allied government had arrived to take their place; thus, the Japanese still occupied Indonesia. Soekarno and other leaders feared provoking the Japanese and at the same time had no assurances that the Allies would not reinstate the Dutch colonial regime. Nevertheless, on August 17, 1945, Soekarno read a sober declaration of independence to a small group in Jakarta, and the sovereign nation of Indonesia was born.

THE WAR FOR INDEPENDENCE

Full independence, however, was not to come to Indonesia for another four years. The Allies finally sent British troops to the islands in late September 1945, but they had no real plan for the nation other than to remove the Japanese and free Europeans from Japanese prisons. In this vacuum, the Dutch reasserted their sovereignty over Indonesia and denounced Soekarno and Hatta as Japanese collaborators. Indonesia tried to set up an Indonesian government, but clashes quickly broke out between the Indonesian army and Japanese and British troops. The fighting escalated, culminating in a ferocious battle in Surabaya in October 1945 that resulted in huge numbers of both British and Indonesian casualties. Because of the fierce resistance shown by Indonesians in this battle, as history scholar M.C. Ricklefs explains, "Surabaya became . . . a national symbol of resistance . . . [and] a rallying-cry for the [Indonesian] Revolution."[9] The British retaliated with air attacks on Surabaya and allowed Dutch troops to land in Java. Together, the Dutch and the British fought a growing armed insurrection by the Indonesian people. Meanwhile, Soekarno's and Hatta's control over the Indonesian government was weakened when Britain promoted a rival, Sutan Sayahir, to become prime minister, or head of the fledgling Indonesian government.

On November 12, 1946, negotiations brokered by the British resulted in the Linggajati Agreement. According to this agreement, the Dutch recognized Indonesia's government, and both sides agreed to work toward allowing the Indonesian government to operate under Dutch oversight. Neither side liked this arrangement, however, and the agreement fell by the wayside almost immediately when the Dutch launched a military action against the Indonesian government in Sumatra and Java in 1947.

Ultimately, another brutal Dutch military action against the Indonesians in 1948, in which Soekarno and Hatta were arrested and exiled, aroused international condemnation. The United Nations Security Council in January 1949 passed a resolution demanding reinstatement of Indonesia's government, and the Dutch were pressured by U.S. and other world leaders to accept the country's independence. The Dutch finally did so on December 27, 1949. Soekarno, the leader of the independence movement since the early 1920s, returned from his second exile and became the first president of a new Republic of Indonesia.

Indonesia's long struggle for independence was over, but it now faced the challenges of coming together as a nation. The new country would now have to manage its own affairs and try to lift its people out of the oppression they had endured at the hands of foreign rulers.

THE ROAD TO DEMOCRACY

Although Indonesia became independent in 1949, it took many more years for the country to move toward unity and democracy. Indeed, these goals were thwarted by authoritarian regimes that used repression to control the country's disparate peoples and secure their own rule. Governmental corruption was commonplace, leaving the Indonesian people to suffer in poverty and hardship. Only recently has Indonesia held fully democratic elections that have given the country new cause for hope.

THE EARLY YEARS OF INDEPENDENCE

Independence did not bring immediate freedom for Indonesians. Instead, the new country entered a period of instability. The years of Dutch colonial rule, Japanese occupation, and war had taken an enormous economic and social toll. Many industries and agricultural plantations had been badly damaged, and Indonesians faced food shortages, unemployment, and worsening poverty. The end of a united resistance to foreign rule also allowed ethnic and religious differences to resurface, and Indonesia's society became very divided. One group of militant Islamic guerrilla fighters, called Darul Islam, even staged a rebellion in West Java against the new government. Meanwhile, the young Indonesian army, which had fought so hard for independence, resisted demobilization and demanded a voice in the new government. In addition, a large number of new political parties, including a reconstituted Indonesian Communist Party (PKI), contributed to growing political instability in Jakarta and the rest of the country.

In the face of these many problems, Soekarno, Indonesia's new president, also had to deal with a parliamentary government system set up under a new constitution that greatly

KAUM BURUH SEDUNIA

President Soekarno addresses an Indonesian Communist party rally in 1965. In the early years of Indonesian independence, membership in the Communist party was very strong.

limited his powers. Under this system, the president was more of a figurehead whose main power was to appoint a cabinet to run the country. Even this action, however, could only be done by negotiating the approval of a parliament, or legislature, made up of representatives from a large number of very different parties. Indonesia, therefore, muddled along in a state of controlled chaos, waiting for Indonesia's first set of elections, which were scheduled for 1955.

Despite the hopes of many Indonesians, however, the 1955 elections did not give Indonesia a stable government. Soekarno's PNI party won the largest number of votes, but so many other parties also won seats in the new parliament that no stable coalition was possible. The weakness of the new government only strengthened growing military dissent. It also encouraged several Islamic separatist movements to wrest power from the government in certain regions of the country. The PKI, Indonesia's Communist party, too, increasingly began to attract a larger and larger following amongst the Indonesian poor since the ineffective government failed to implement sound economic policies. As social scientist Seekins explains, "The result [of the 1955 elections] was chronic instability . . . that eroded the foundations of the parliamentary system."[10]

Finally, in 1956, Soekarno tired of the difficulties of the parliamentary system and began to advocate a more authoritarian style of government that he called "Guided Democracy." Under this plan, which Soekarno described as more aligned with the traditional Indonesian village system of discussion and consensus, the divisions in parliament would be remedied by giving the president—like a village chieftain—much greater power to guide and shape government policy. In protest of Soekarno's grab for power, Vice President Hatta resigned, and his supporters in Sumatra staged a rebellion that tried to take the government back from Soekarno. Soekarno, however, put down the revolt by aligning with the military and declaring martial law. In 1959, Soekarno completed his quest for real power by overthrowing the parliament and reinstating the 1945 constitution, which favored a strong presidency. In 1960, a new legislature, called the House of People's Representatives (DPR), was established, and the majority of its seats were appointed by Soekarno. Most of these were assigned to military leaders and the PKI, with whom Soekarno had established a governing coalition. Islamic forces and those associated with Sumatra's rebellion were largely excluded from the government. Soekarno continued as president and later even proclaimed himself "President for Life."

SOEKARNO'S AUTHORITARIAN REGIME

Soekarno's authoritarian rule, however, only further bankrupted a country already impoverished by centuries of colonialism, occupation, and war. Soekarno ignored economic advice provided by advisers within his country and from U.S. and international economic experts. Instead, he spent the country's limited funds on expensive public monuments, lavish palaces, and government buildings that were meant to exalt the new country's greatness. In fact, Richard Nixon, who later became president of the United States, visited Indonesia during the 1960s and commented on Soekarno's expenditures: "In no other country we visited was the conspicuous luxury of the ruler in such striking contrast to the poverty and misery of his people. Jakarta was a collection of sweltering huts and hovels. . . . But Soekarno's palace was painted a spotless white and set in the middle of hundreds of acres of exotic gardens."[11] As a result of Soekarno's decisions, Indonesia's economy grew worse, and ordinary Indonesians continued to suffer from food shortages and increasing inflation of prices.

Soekarno's rule also resulted in an aggressive foreign policy that soon alienated the United States and Western governments. Soekarno's first target was the island of New Guinea. Soekarno considered the western side of the island (which Indonesians called Irian Barat) part of Indonesia, but the Dutch had continued to occupy it even after Indonesia's declaration of independence. Relying on his army, Soekarno began a series of diplomatic and military confrontations with the Dutch over the area. Soekarno eventually seized the region, with United Nations (UN) approval, in 1963. (In 1972, it was made a province of Indonesia and renamed Irian Jaya, meaning victorious Irian.)

Later in 1963, Soekarno initiated a confrontation with the new nation of Malaysia. Parts of Borneo, which bordered Indonesia's Kalimantan region, were undecided about whether to join Malaysia. Hoping to add to Indonesia's territory, Soekarno sought to encourage a revolution among these people and sent Indonesia's army to stage offensives along the Kalimantan-Malaysia border. These military posturings were easily defeated by British forces stationed in Borneo, but Soekarno's actions alarmed the United States and other countries and led to a cessation of much of Indonesia's foreign aid at the same time as Indonesia was increasing its defense spending. These two trends depleted Indonesia's revenues and only further deepened its economic troubles.

Soekarno's policies also resulted in continuing political instability within Indonesia. The PKI, under Soekarno, became stronger, and by 1965, it was the largest Communist party in the world, except for the Communists in the Soviet Union and China—the countries where the ideology of communism was founded. The PKI pushed for and won, with Soekarno's support, many social reforms designed to redistribute land to Indonesian peasants and improve living conditions for the poor. The Communists' growing influence within the government, however, eventually threatened the army, the other major part of Soekarno's power base. In 1963, the PKI made a fateful decision to enforce land reforms in

Java and Bali by taking land from landlords and distributing it to peasants. These actions led to violent clashes between peasants and landowners, as well as to PKI confrontations with the army when it tried to put down the revolts. The army became even more disgruntled with Soekarno and the PKI in 1965, when the PKI sought to create a "fifth force" of armed peasants and workers, and received an offer of arms from Indonesia's then ally, Communist China.

The hostilities between the PKI and the army soon spelled the beginning of the end for Soekarno's rule. In 1965, an attempted coup almost succeeded in disrupting Soekarno's hold on power. Although no one knows for certain, many have alleged that the coup was staged by a Communist faction or even by the PKI itself. Nevertheless, the coup was thwarted with the help of General Soeharto, the head of Indonesia's army.

Following the coup attempt, Soeharto presided over a massive purge of Communists throughout the country. The purge killed as many as five hundred thousand people, imprisoned thousands more, and eliminated the PKI as a force in Indonesian politics. As historians Robert Cribb and Colin Brown explain, "By the end of [1965], an extended series of massacres was taking place throughout the country, with the

In 1967 General Soeharto staged a successful military coup against President Soekarno and implemented an authoritarian regime that Soeharto called the "New Order."

killing concentrated where the PKI had once been strongest: in the countryside of Java and Bali and on the plantations of North Sumatra. . . . Further outbreaks continued until 1969."[12] Much of the slaughter was carried out by civilian mobs in Java and Bali who were opposed to the PKI's ideas and actions, but the military encouraged and supported the mass executions; it even participated by helping to find Communists in hiding. As the purges continued, Soeharto consolidated his control over the army and maneuvered to remove Soekarno from power. On March 12, 1967, Soekarno was officially ousted and Soeharto was named Indonesia's acting president.

SOEHARTO'S "NEW ORDER" GOVERNMENT

Soeharto's government, which he dubbed the "New Order," claimed that it would reform politics in Indonesia. In the end, however, Soeharto reinstated the same type of authoritarian control that was exercised by Soekarno and offered Indonesians only a continuation of the repressive policies of the previous regime. First, he slowly but surely eliminated all vestiges of Soekarno's government and replaced Soekarno's appointments with people he could trust. Soeharto gave the army a much larger role in government, and he used it to enforce his decisions and monitor the activities of government officials and civilians. Most political parties were eliminated; only two were allowed to survive—the Partai Persatuan Pembangunan (PPP), which consisted of all Islamic groups, and Partai Demokrasi Indonesia (PDI), Soekarno's old party. Both were forced to declare their support for the New Order government. In addition, a new government-sanctioned party was created called Golkar, which came to be the only real party with power under Soeharto. Some people protested for greater political freedom, but these uprisings were quickly repressed and their leaders put in jail for sedition. Elections were held several times during Soeharto's rule, but most observers agree that they were carefully staged only to create an appearance of democracy.

However, Indonesia under Soeharto began to prosper economically due, at least in part, to the relative political stability brought by his authoritarian rule. One of Soeharto's first steps was to restore relations with the United States and other Western countries. Renewing these relationships, in

turn, helped to bring much-needed foreign aid and economic advice from international financial entities such as the World Bank and the International Monetary Fund (IMF). Following this advice, the government restructured the country's large foreign debt, restrained government spending, and passed laws to encourage foreign investment. In addition, between 1969 and the 1990s, Indonesia implemented a series of five-year plans that increased production of staple foods, repaired the country's infrastructure (including roads, ports, and electric facilities), developed agriculture and basic industries, and improved transportation and communications. As a result of these initiatives, Indonesia's economy rebounded. Food and health care became more available, employment increased, and government revenues expanded. Oil production was one of the most important generators of this economic expansion; Indonesia benefited greatly from a rise in prices following a 1973 oil embargo by Mideast oil-producing nations.

Unfortunately, this economic boom also created fertile ground for government corruption that flourished under Soeharto's rule. As economist Richard Robinson explained in a 1978 article, "Powerful public figures, especially in the military, gained control of potentially lucrative offices and used them as personal fiefs. . . not only to build private economic empires but also to consolidate and enhance their political power."[13] The breadth of this corruption was revealed in the

Under Soeharto, the economy of Indonesia expanded, mostly due to rising profits from the production of oil in the 1970s.

INDEPENDENCE FOR EAST TIMOR

The island of Timor, located in Nusa Tenggara, was originally claimed by both the Portuguese and the Dutch. In 1859, the two nations agreed to divide the island, with Portuguese rule in the east and Dutch rule in the west. The Dutch half became part of Indonesia in 1949, but East Timor did not begin to fight for independence from Portugal until 1974. In 1975, with East Timor in a state of civil war, Indonesia invaded, claiming sovereignty over the entire island. Indonesia's military brutally suppressed local insurgents, in the process killing or starving more than one hundred thousand civilians. East Timor was declared a province of Indonesia in 1976. The international community, however, refused to recognize Indonesia's sovereignty, and after many decades of unrest, Indonesia agreed that the East Timorese could vote on whether they wanted independence. In the referendum conducted by the United Nations (UN) in 1999, almost 80 percent voted for independence. Unfortunately, the vote caused militia groups linked to the Indonesia military to go on a bloody rampage that killed about one hundred thousand independence supporters. UN troops were sent to maintain order, however, and the first presidential elections were successfully held in April 2002.

Ecstatic residents of East Timor celebrate after their country gained independence from Indonesian rule in 2002.

1970s when General Ibnu Sutowo, head of the government-owned oil enterprise Pertamina, was forced to resign after it was discovered that his corrupt management had run up a debt of $10 billion. The company's near collapse threatened the country's fragile economy.

Soeharto, like Soekarno, also sought to maintain and expand Indonesia's borders through military force. In Irian Jaya, which had been annexed by Indonesia in 1963, and Aceh, the northern region of Sumatra, the government put down uprisings of local guerrilla fighters resistant to Indonesian rule. In 1975, the Indonesian army reacted similarly to separatists in East Timor who sought independence from Portugal, which had long maintained a colony on the island. When civil war broke out in 1975, Indonesian troops invaded East Timor, and the following year the government declared East Timor part of Indonesia. When resistance continued, Indonesian troops, throughout the late 1970s and 1980s, carried out a brutal program of military occupation, mass starvation, and disease that sought to subdue the separatists but also killed over 200,000 of East Timor's 650,000 inhabitants. The military campaign brought Indonesia international criticism for its blatant violation of human rights. In fact, the UN steadfastly refused to recognize Indonesia's sovereignty over East Timor, until finally, with UN protection, the people of the region finally achieved independence from Indonesia in 2002.

THE 1997 ECONOMIC CRISIS AND SOEHARTO'S FALL

Soeharto's New Order policies, over time, began to create deep resentments among the Indonesian people. The poor were happy to see some improvements in their lives as a result of economic growth, but at the same time they watched a minority of Indonesians grow very rich from widespread corruption. It was obvious to all that Soeharto's family and friends, in particular, acquired great wealth. Islamic sectors of the population, meanwhile, became disenchanted with the government's secular, nonreligious outlook, even in traditionally sacred rites such as marriage. Many Indonesians also worried that the increasing amounts of foreign investment and influence would lead to a westernization of Indonesian culture. Increasing numbers of people, too, resented the lack of political freedom and the inflated role of the military in Indonesian affairs.

Many of these concerns were at the forefront of violent demonstrations that broke out in Jakarta in 1974 during the visit of a Japanese prime minister. These demonstrations, later called the Malari riots, involved tens of thousands of students who looted and set fires throughout the city. The military eventually stopped the rioting, but only after eleven demonstrators were killed. The government's response to the

Police in riot gear beat students demonstrating near the presidential palace in Jakarta. Since the late 1990s, Indonesian students have staged several protests against the government.

uprising was to increase the government's restrictions on freedom of expression by banning public meetings, closing newspapers and magazines, and generally increasing government repression. Popular dissatisfaction with Soeharto's regime, therefore, remained underground for many more years, and Soeharto continued in power even as he aged into his seventies.

Indonesians' deep frustrations with Soeharto finally overflowed in July 1997, when an Asian financial crisis destroyed Indonesia's economy. The IMF offered aid but tied it to austere economic reforms that resulted in cutbacks of government subsidies to the poor and increases in fuel and electricity prices. These rising prices sparked widespread rioting and rebellion by Indonesians already hit by the monetary crisis. Much of this anger was directed at a minority ethnic group, the Chinese, whose successful businesses were heavily looted. The rippling effects of the crisis quickly decimated Indonesia's economy. By 1998, a number of banks collapsed, businesses went bankrupt, millions lost their jobs, and gains achieved in combating poverty were reversed overnight.

At the end of the millennium, Indonesia was in a state of anarchy, with rioting and protests raging throughout the archipelago. There were constant demands for Soeharto's resignation. In one of the worst disturbances, for example, soldiers shot four students during demonstrations in May 1998 in Jakarta, and the city erupted in fierce violence. As travel writer Turner describes, "In three days of rioting and looting, over 2000 buildings in Jakarta were damaged or destroyed, and an estimated 1200 people died, mostly those trapped in burning shopping centers. Ordinary people, the urban poor, joined in the looting as law and order collapsed."[14] In the face of these events, on May 21, 1998, after thirty-two years of rule, Soeharto stepped down, and his vice president, B.J. Habibie, was installed as president.

THE RISE OF DEMOCRACY IN INDONESIA

As soon as he was made president, Habibie promised political reforms, democratic elections, and an end to corruption. Indonesians enthusiastically supported what they hoped would be a new, more open era in the country's politics. As time passed, however, Habibie appeared to continue Soeharto's reliance on the army and seemed to be stalling on setting a date for democratic elections. Indonesians quickly became disenchanted with Habibie, and protests and violence again erupted around the country. Protesters demanded immediate elections and the removal of military appointees from parliament. Pressured by these events, Habibie scheduled elections for June 1999.

Finally, in 1999, Indonesia held its first truly democratic elections. Abdurrahman Wahid, a nearly blind and physically infirm Muslim scholar who had widespread popular support, became Indonesia's first democratically elected president. Wahid, however, rapidly lost the confidence of Indonesia's parliament, which impeached him and removed him from office after just twenty months in power. Lawmakers accused Wahid of political incompetence and involvement in government corruption following two financial scandals concerning embezzled state funds and missing humanitarian aid moneys. In 2001, Wahid was replaced by his vice president, Megawati Soekarnoputri, the daughter of Indonesia's founding president, Soekarno.

Megawati helped restore social stability and won high marks internationally for her efforts to spur economic growth. Under her watch, inflation and public debt both decreased significantly, and Indonesia's economy grew at a rate of about 3 to 4 percent per year—still not enough to provide enough jobs, but a big improvement for the country. Megawati, however, began to lose support among many Indonesians who were facing continuing poverty, and she was widely criticized for failing to combat the deep government corruption that had plagued the country's government for so long.

PRESIDENT YUDHOYONO

Susilo Bambang Yudhoyono was elected president of Indonesia in 2004. He was born on September 9, 1949, in East Java, the son of an army officer. He, too, became an army officer. A graduate of the Indonesian Military Academy, he took part in the Indonesian invasion of East Timor in 1975. During the 1980s, Yudhoyono studied in the United States, earning a master's degree in business management. He later earned a PhD in agricultural economics. After returning to Indonesia, Yudhoyono held various military commands before finally retiring from the military in April 2000. That same year, Yudhoyono began his political career. As minister for security and political affairs under President Wahid, he worked to reform the military and get the army out of politics. In 2001, Wahid, facing impeachment, asked Yudhoyono to declare a state of emergency. Yudhoyono's refusal cemented his reputa-

tion as a reformer and independent thinker. After Wahid was removed, Indonesia's new president, Megawati Soekarnoputri, reappointed Yudhoyono as security minister. In this position, Yudhoyono supervised the hunt for the terrorists responsible for the 2002 Bali bombing. In March 2004, Yudhoyono resigned and began his run for the presidency, winning that office in September 2004.

Former security minister Susilo Bambang Yudhoyono became president of Indonesia in September 2004.

In the next set of elections, in September 2004, 80 percent of Indonesian voters turned out to vote in the country's first direct presidential ballot. Until this time, voters elected representatives for the country's supreme parliament, called the People's Consultative Assembly, or MPR, and the MPR then chose the president by majority vote. In 2001, however, the parliament passed a law providing for the direct elections, by popular vote, of the president and vice president. In the 2004 elections, the first elections conducted under this new system, no one candidate won at least 50 percent of the vote, so a run-off election had to be held between the top vote-getters—among them Megawati and Susilo Bambang Yudhoyono, a retired general with an American education who had been Megawati's former national security adviser. In this run-off election, Yudhoyono won by a landslide, becoming Indonesia's new president.

President Yudhoyono earned early praise for his promises to clean up corruption, rein in the military, install an independent judiciary, and foster greater economic development. His leadership was soon severely tested, as the giant tsunami hit Indonesia and several other neighboring countries on December 26, 2004, creating vast devastation and leaving hundreds of thousands dead, missing, injured, orphaned, or homeless. As 2005 began, Yudhoyono faced not only the task of healing the country from this catastrophic natural disaster, but also many other challenges, including maintaining forward economic progress, rooting out government corruption, combating poverty, and addressing continuing ethnic, religious, and social divisions throughout the archipelago.

No one knows for certain what this next chapter of democracy will bring for Indonesia, but few can doubt that the country in recent years has made major strides in overthrowing tyranny and repression. If a stable and honest democratic system of government can be established, observers believe that the Indonesian people will at last have a strong voice in choosing their destiny.

4

INDONESIAN SOCIETY

Indonesia's settlement history and geography have created a land of great social diversity in which hundreds of very different ethnic groups exist side by side. As the British Broadcasting Corporation (BBC) Web site explains, "The people [of Indonesia] range from stone-age hunter-gatherers to a modern urban elite."[15] Despite the government's efforts to meld these disparate groups into one unified country, the differences among Indonesians have historically contributed to deep social and religious conflicts.

A DIVERSE POPULATION

Not only was Indonesia settled by peoples who migrated from various parts of the world, but its rugged mountains and numerous small islands separated these settlements from one another. As a result, Indonesia today comprises an incredible variety of ethnic groups, languages, religions, and cultural traditions. According to one classification, for example, Indonesia is home to as many as three hundred ethnic groups who speak some 365 languages. In fact, as travel writer Turner explains, "Indonesia's national motto is 'Bhinneka Tunggal Ika,' an old Javanese phrase meaning 'They are many, they are one,' which usually gets translated as 'Unity in Diversity.'"[16]

Most Indonesians today are of Malay ancestry—descendants of early peoples who migrated from China and Indochina. Most of this majority Malay population lives on Indonesia's larger islands (Java, Sumatra, Kalimantan, and Sulawesi) and Bali. These groups historically have had considerable interaction with outsiders, mainly through tourism and commerce, and tend to be familiar with the modern world.

However, numerous distinctive tribes, who follow various religions and speak many different languages and dialects, can still be found among Indonesia's numerous islands. These include isolated groups who have had little contact with outsiders even to this day. For example, the Kubu tribe of south Sumatra, the Papuan Dani people of the Baliem Valley in Irian Jaya, the Badui of West Java, and the Dayaks from the interior of Kalimantan are all relatively primitive peoples who live very traditional lives removed from most of Indonesian and global society.

A MUSLIM COUNTRY

Not surprisingly, in light of its numerous cultures, Indonesia is home to several different religions. However, Indonesia is the largest Islamic nation in the world. Eighty-eight percent of the people follow the Islamic faith. Other religions, such as Christianity, Hinduism, and Buddhism, are followed by much smaller numbers of Indonesians. Although religion plays a very significant role in the lives of most Indonesians, the government has historically tried to remain secular, or

An Indonesian tribesman poses for a picture. Primitive tribes still lead traditional lives on the more remote islands of Indonesia, having little contact with outsiders.

Muslims bow in prayer outside a large mosque in Banda Aceh. Indonesia has the largest Islamic population in the world.

nonreligious, in its policies. For example, the country's founding principles, the Pancasila, include a general belief in God yet at the same time do not advocate a state religion. Instead, religious tolerance is a key part of the country's national creed and constitution.

Followers of Islam, called Muslims, believe in one God, called Allah, and follow the teachings of the Koran, Islam's holy book. Throughout the world, Islam is split into two branches—the Sunnis and the Shia—but most of Indonesia's Muslims are Sunni.

Many of Indonesia's Muslims, however, are very different from Muslims in other parts of the world. Although Indonesians typically follow certain Islamic customs, such as avoiding alcohol and drugs and not eating pork, the majority of Indonesian Muslims practice a generally tolerant and moderate version of Islam. Muslim women in Indonesia, for example, are usually allowed much more freedom than those in Mideastern societies; for example, they do not have to cover their heads with the traditional Islamic headscarf, called the *jilbab*, or remain segregated from men in their activities. Certain Indonesian Muslims in Sumatra even allow matriarchal, or female, rule, whereas Islam traditionally views males as the superior and dominant sex. Many parts of Indonesia, in fact, believe in the very nontraditional form of Islam called Kejawen, or Kebatinan, which incorporates Hindu, Buddhist, and animist beliefs with Islamic customs. President Soeharto, for example, was a believer in this form of Islam. At the same time, a growing minority of Indonesians do follow more orthodox versions of Islam. Aceh, in northern Sumatra, for example, is a stronghold for a highly conservative version of Islam.

Christianity was first introduced to the islands by the Portuguese and the Dutch in the sixteenth and seventeenth centuries. In later centuries, Christian missionaries brought many different Christian sects to Indonesia, including those of the Catholic and Lutheran churches. Today, most Christians in Indonesia are of Protestant denominations, such as the Lutherans, and these practitioners are concentrated in areas of Sumatra, Irian Jaya, Maluku, Kalimantan, Tengah, and Sulawesi. Catholics tend to be grouped in parts of Kalimantan, Irian Jaya, and Nusa Tenggara. Most Muslims and Christians get along with each other, but in recent years incidents of religious violence have become a problem.

Hinduism, a religion brought to Indonesia from India, is mostly found on the island of Bali, where Hindus form approximately 93 percent of the population. A few other Hindu enclaves, however, are scattered throughout the rest of the country. Balinese Hinduism is somewhat different from Indian Hinduism. In traditional Indian Hinduism, the physical world is considered to be an illusion, and the meaninglessness of "things" is a lesson that must be learned by each person through a cycle of reincarnations until he or she can rise above the physical plane of existence. Balinese Hindus have largely substituted a belief in ancestral spirits for the ideas of rebirth and reincarnation. Also, Hindus in Bali concentrate their energies on one god, Shiva, instead of worshipping three gods—Brahma, Shiva, and Vishnu—as traditional Hindus do. The Balinese hold many beautiful and artistic rituals and ceremonies to appease the spirit world and court the favor of specific spirits during important life events, such as puberty, marriage, and cremation at death.

Buddhism came to Indonesia from both India and China. The religion is really more of a philosophy, founded on the principle that life's suffering can be overcome by overcoming desire, with the ultimate goal of nirvana, or enlightenment, which brings complete freedom from suffering and pain. Buddhism usually does not emphasize belief in particular gods, but in Indonesia, to satisfy the Pancasila principle of belief in one god, Buddhism was adapted to recognize a single deity, Sang Hyan Adi Buddha, giving the religion a uniquely Indonesian flavor. Most declared Buddhists in Indonesia today are members of its Chinese minority, who mix Buddhist ideas with other traditional Chinese beliefs. Although Buddhism does not require attendance at a temple, Indonesia has many beautiful Buddhist pagodas and temples where worshippers can meditate.

THE JAVANESE, SUNDANESE, MADURESE, AND MALAYS

Despite Indonesia's great social and religious diversity, the majority of Indonesia's population is made up of four main ethnic groups—the Javanese, the Sundanese, the Madurese, and the coastal Malays—all of whom follow the Islamic religion. Most of these peoples also live on the island of Java, except for coastal Malays who live on the coasts of Sumatra.

Of the country's major ethnic groups, the Javanese are the most numerous and tend to dominate the national culture. Most live in east and central Java in small, rice-growing villages. In these communities, there is a strong tradition of cooperation among neighbors in order to complete rice harvests and other work projects, provide security, and manage other aspects of life. Village society places a high value on children, and parents tend to be very indulgent with youngsters. As their child grows, parents become increasingly disciplinarian in order to teach the complex rules of Javan society. These rules emphasize respect for elders and persons of status, proper etiquette and politeness, and formality with strangers.

In fact, the Javanese language even contains various speech "levels" that reflect different degrees of formality as well as the social status of the person being addressed. Thus, a Javanese speaker must decide whether a social situation is formal or informal, and evaluate whom they are talking with, and then choose the correct words to fit the occasion and the audience. Most Javanese also follow a very moderate version of Islam mixed with Hindu-Buddhist influences and indigenous animist beliefs in spirits. These beliefs are often

INDONESIAN ETIQUETTE

Despite recent developments and changes in society, Indonesia remains a very traditional country. Throughout Indonesia, family values and religion are important. Children are expected to be respectful to parents and elders, and Western ideas of individualism are seen as less important than the concerns of the family or village. Also, Indonesians are typically polite and careful not to offend. Near tourist areas, local people are more tolerant, but visitors can benefit from following a few rules of Indonesian etiquette:

1. It is impolite to use the left hand to give or receive objects. The left hand is used to wash after going to the toilet and is viewed as unclean.

2. Hospitality is highly valued, and it is considered impolite to refuse an offer of food or drink.

3. It is customary to shake hands with everyone in the room when arriving or leaving a social situation.

4. Avoid touching Indonesians on the head. It is considered the seat of the soul among some cultures.

5. Talking to someone with your hands on your hips is a sign to Indonesians of contempt, anger, or aggression.

expressed in feasts, visits to shrines and temples, offerings to spirits, and use of spiritual healers. Pockets of East Java, however, follow more fundamental Islamic teachings.

The Sundanese, another populous ethnic group, are very similar to the Javanese in their culture and lifestyle. They live mostly in small villages in West Java and, like the Javanese, many are rice farmers. However, the Sundanese speak an entirely different language, called Sunda, are less refined and formal in their use of language and etiquette, and tend to have much stronger ties to Islam. At the same time, many Sundanese share some of the Javanese beliefs in animist spirits.

Indonesia's third largest ethnic group, the Madurese, live near the city of Surabaya on the northern coast of East Java and on the nearby island of Madura. This area is a center for fundamental Islam. Most Madurese are devout Muslims who live in villages that function around a religious center. Like

Javanese farmers tend to rice plants in a paddy in central Java. The Javanese are the largest major ethnic group in Indonesia.

other Muslims in Indonesia, however, the Madurese also practice certain forms of animism. The Madurese work as farmers, animal herders, or fishermen, and are known among other Indonesians as earthy, hotheaded, and sometimes violent. As the Joshua Project Web site reports, "Bull racing and blood feuds are central aspects of [Madurese] culture. They are also known for seeking out 'blood revenge' in cases of adultery and cattle theft, or incidences involving public shame."[17]

A fourth sizable Indonesian ethnic group, known as the coastal Malays, are people of Malaysian stock who speak the Malay language and live near the coasts of northern Sumatra. Like many other Indonesians, they grow rice, fish, and live in small villages. Also, like many Indonesians, they are Muslims who generally follow the Islamic faith mixed with aspects of animist beliefs. Courtesy and politeness are important to this culture, too, although their family and social ties are not as rigidly structured. Many traditional Malay crafts, such as the making of batik cloth, are still practiced in the coastal villages.

THE BALINESE
Apart from the four main ethnic groups, Indonesia is made up of hundreds of smaller ethnicities. One of the most well-known of these groups is the Balinese, who live in numerous

small villages on Bali and nearby Lombok, two small islands just south of Java.

In contrast to the Javanese and similar ethnic groups, who lean toward refinement, modesty, and formality, the people of Bali are known for their earthiness and friendliness. As travel writer Dalton explains, "The Balinese are an extraordinarily creative people with a highly sensual, theatrical culture. . . . [They] prefer the headier, flashier sensations—laughs, terror, spicier and sweeter foods. They're more lavish . . . in their colors and decorations; they like explosive music and fast, jerky dancing."[18] The Balinese are also unlike many other Indonesians because they follow the Hindu religion rather than Islam. The unique and colorful Balinese version of Hinduism permeates all parts of life in Bali. Almost every village has a temple, and people make daily offerings to the gods and participate in many religious events. The Balinese also have very

Balinese women carry fruits and flowers on their heads at the opening of a festival in 2003. Of Indonesia's many ethnic groups, the Balinese are the best known.

complex and highly structured social ties. People in Bali are extremely loyal to their families and their home villages, and they participate in most activities as part of a carefully organized and shared community effort.

Perhaps the most notable part of traditional Bali society, however, is its Hindu caste system, in which the caste, or social level, a person is born into determines a person's opportunities and lifestyle. Although Bali's caste system is much more relaxed than India's, and many younger people today even ignore it, traces of its influence on the organization of Balinese society persist. For example, higher caste members expect to be given respect from the lower castes, and people are still sometimes expected to marry within their castes in order not to upset the social order.

SUMATRA'S ETHNIC GROUPS

Several very distinct ethnic groups can also be found on the island of Sumatra. One of these is the Acehnese from northern Sumatra. The Aceh area of Sumatra has a long history of trade, and as Arab traders and scholars traveled there, it became an early stronghold for Islam in Indonesia. Aceh became wealthy due to its trading activities, and it managed to remain independent of Dutch rule for many decades. Though Aceh was finally occupied in 1871, the Acehnese conducted a thirty-five-year guerrilla war against the Dutch that destabilized the foreigners' control of the region. After Indonesia achieved independence in 1949, when the Indonesian government used armed troops to annex the area as part of the new country, the Acehnese similarly resisted Indonesian rule. Today, the continuing conflict is one of Indonesia's most vexing social problems.

Sumatra has two other distinctive ethnic groups—the Batak from the interior forests of North Sumatra, and the Minangkabau from West Sumatra. The Batak are primarily Muslim farmers who live in the highlands around Lake Toba and Samosir Island. Their society is organized according to a male descent system, called *marga*, and is based on land ownership. Each marga owns a portion of land and functions as an extended family. Young men take wives from a different marga and the wife then joins the man's marga.

In stark contrast to the Batak, the Minangkabau are famous in Indonesia for their matrilineal social system. Under

VIOLENCE IN ACEH

The relationship between Aceh (part of northern Sumatra) and the government of Indonesia has always been rocky. Aceh became a province of the country at the time of independence, but has always sought to remain fairly independent of the central government. During President Soekarno's regime, an armed rebellion called Darul Islam (House of Islam) arose seeking to establish an Islamic state in Aceh. The modern independence movement began in 1976, when the Free Aceh movement (GAM) was formed. The Indonesian government was able to suppress the group for many years, but it reemerged in 1989 and has been at war with government troops ever since. During the 1990s, one thousand to three thousand people were killed, many more were injured, and many civilian homes were burned to the ground. Rebels accuse the Indonesian military of murder, torture, rape, and other human rights violations. A peace agreement was negotiated in 2002 providing for autonomy and free elections in Aceh in exchange for disarmament by rebels, but talks broke down. Martial law was then imposed, closing the area to outsiders. The rebels' main complaint is that the Indonesian government exploits the rich natural resources of Aceh, leaving local people in poverty.

Indonesian police aim their weapons at a band of GAM militants in Aceh.

this system, all property is inherited by women, and children are considered to be descended from mothers instead of fathers. Despite the prominence and power given to women in this society, however, the Minangkabau, like the Batak, are strongly Islamic. Men simply have their own sphere of influence, often involving business and moneymaking, while women control the family and the distribution and cultivation of land.

INDONESIA'S CHINESE MINORITY

One of Indonesia's smallest ethnic groups is the Chinese, who are settled throughout the nation's various islands. The Chinese are descendants of Chinese traders who first came to Indonesia's islands centuries ago. During Dutch rule, they acted as middlemen between the Dutch rulers and the Indonesian people, a role for which they were greatly resented. Hostility toward this group also increased after the Communist purge of Indonesia, because many Chinese sympathized with the Communists.

In modern times, many Chinese continued to work as businessmen or retail shop owners, often prospering economically. A few even grew quite wealthy, becoming Indonesia's richest families, a development that has stirred even more resentment among other ethnic groups. Over the years, this hostility against the Chinese minority has surfaced in killings, lootings, and burnings of Chinese houses and businesses, as well as in government restrictions that outlawed the Chinese language and culture.

The rioting that erupted during the fall of Soeharto in 1998 included brutal attacks on Chinese communities and caused many wealthier Chinese to flee Indonesia and take their money with them. Recent Indonesian leaders, however, have abolished discriminatory laws, called for ethnic tolerance, and urged the Chinese to return to Indonesia.

THE PUSH FOR A NATIONAL IDENTITY

Recognizing the political challenges posed by so many disparate peoples, the government of Indonesia has long tried to unite the country's many ethnic and religious groups to create a national Indonesian identity. When independence was first declared in 1949, Indonesia was merely a collection of hundreds of different societies, united mainly by their hatred of the Dutch. Through the principles of Pancasila, Soekarno began the process of trying to meld the many Indonesian societies into one nation. Since then, each of Indonesia's leaders has tried to continue this process of integration.

One of the central tools for building a national identity was through the spread of Bahasa Indonesian, a language closely related to Malay that was designated as the country's official language. This language is taught in Indonesian schools, used in government activities and in newspapers and other publications, and relied upon as a means of communication among different ethnic groups. As a result, most Indonesians today speak Bahasa Indonesian as well as their ethnic or local tongue.

Other government methods of integration have included teaching national unity in educational curricula and creating national holidays and celebrations to bring people together as one nation. Perhaps the most effective method, however, was the government's strict control and censorship of media such as television, newspapers, movies, and literature. Throughout the Soeharto period, Indonesia's laws prohibited discussion of topics that might be socially divisive. These prohibited topics were known by the acronym SARA—*suku* (ethnicity), *agama* (religion), *ras* (race), and *antargolongan* (social relations). People who violated these laws could have their work privileges revoked or their businesses shut down by the government. Through state-owned broadcasting, the government also produced positive media content that promoted its ideals of a stable and unified Indonesian society.

THE CRISIS IN IRIAN JAYA

Like their counterparts in East Timor and Aceh, rebels in Irian Jaya have been fighting for decades for independence. Irian Jaya is Indonesia's official name for the western half of the large island of New Guinea, an area also called Papua. Once part of the Dutch colonial empire, the region was temporarily administered by the United Nations (UN) after the Dutch withdrew. It became a province of Indonesia in the 1960s, through a referendum process that many countries protested as invalid; afterward the fight for independence was begun by the Free Papua Movement (*Organisasi Papua Merdeka* or OPM). Over the years, the people of Irian Jaya have suffered greatly from the conflict. As in East Timor, Indonesian troops have been accused of numerous human rights violations, including shootings of peaceful demonstrators, torture, arbitrary detention, and the use of air attacks and napalm on rural villages. The total number of civilians killed is unknown, but some observers estimate the figure at more than one hundred thousand. In recent years, the Indonesian government tried to negotiate with OPM, but talks ended in 2001 when troops murdered separatist leader Theys Eluay. Since then relations have been worsening.

SOCIAL AND RELIGIOUS CONFLICTS

Observers have suggested, however, that the Indonesian government's heavy-handed attempts to impose a national identity may have created only an attractive veneer to hide simmering divisions within Indonesian society. Indeed, since the fall of Soeharto, social and religious conflicts have become increasingly apparent. These conflicts pit Muslims against other Muslims, Muslims against Christians and Hindus, rural peasants against city dwellers, rich against poor, and various separatist cultures against the idea of a united Indonesia. Today, separatist movements continue in two parts of the country—the Free Aceh Movement on Sumatra and the Free Papua Movement, a rebel group in Irian Jaya. Both movements are seeking to carve independent states out of the Indonesian collective.

In addition, more fundamental and radical Islamic elements have increasingly gained strength since 1998. Islamic political parties, which both Soekarno and Soeharto tried to suppress, have multiplied in the new millennium, and fundamentalist Islam has blossomed. Signs of this turn toward more conservative Islam include the fact that more women are covering their heads with the traditional jilbab scarf, more people are making annual Muslim pilgrimages to Mecca, and some areas, such as Aceh, have even adopted *sharia*, or Islamic law—a strict code of behavior and justice that would never have been tolerated by previous Indonesian rulers.

With the rise of fundamentalist Islam, Muslim extremist groups have gained strength in Indonesia. These groups are behind much of the nation's anti-Christian violence, and they are responsible for several major terrorist attacks against Western targets in the country. The most infamous attack occurred in Bali in October 2002. In this incident, two bars frequented by Western tourists were bombed by Islamic terrorists, killing 202 people and injuring another 209. The militant terrorist group Jemaah Islamiyah was found responsible. The bombings remain the worst instances of terrorism in Indonesia's history.

Religious separatism, terrorism, and independence movements reveal that Indonesia still faces a struggle to unite its diverse peoples under one national banner. Indeed, as the country moves toward greater democracy and less repression, managing social conflicts has become one of the country's most important challenges.

A MIX OF CULTURES

Although Indonesia's multiple ethnicities and religious differences are responsible for many divisions within Indonesian society, this same diversity has also contributed to a fantastic array of cultures, each with its own manner of artistic expression. Although Javanese and Balinese arts are dominant, the country's many different peoples and cultural influences all contribute to a rich, robust, and highly unique Indonesian culture.

THEATER AND DANCE FROM JAVA AND BALI

The most well-known Indonesian arts among westerners are from Java and Bali. One of the most famous of these arts, for example, is an ancient tradition of storytelling called shadow puppet shows. These shows, which have long been popular among tourists, originated in ancient times and often convey age-old myths. The highly skilled puppet master, called a *dalang*, works behind a backlit screen so that only the shadows of the puppets are visible to the audience. In addition to working the puppets, the dalang supplies the voices of the various characters, tells jokes, and sometimes sings. The performances can last as long as nine hours and are accompanied by traditional music.

The most common type of shadow shows are called *wayang kulit* and feature intricate two-dimensional puppets similar to paper dolls, which are made in stylized human shapes out of goatskin with movable limbs. The Sundanese in West Java, however, produce shows that use three-dimensional wooden puppets with painted faces and decorations, called *wayang golek*. The shadow plays are performed in villages and towns on public holidays, during religious festivals, as well as for family events such as weddings, birth celebrations, circumcisions, and cremations.

Indonesia is also known around the world for its traditional Balinese dances, which are also heavily influenced by Hindu myths and culture. These dances are a central part of

Balinese dancers pose in expressive masks and elaborate costumes before a performance of the traditional wayang wong dance.

Balinese life and are performed regularly in the villages of Bali, where they are incorporated into religious ceremonies or are used to entertain family and friends. Balinese dances fall into one of three categories: *Wali*, sacred dances that can only be performed inside a temple; *Beboli*, ceremonial dances; and *Balih-balihan*, dances performed solely for entertainment. Among these dances, a ceremonial dance drama called *Gambuh* is one of the oldest. It tells the story of a Javanese prince who is searching for his beautiful princess. Another classic Balinese dance, this one performed primarily for entertainment, is the dance of *Lelong*, a very feminine dance typically performed by two young girls. Yet another popular dance is the *wayang wong*, a drama in which masked dancers play the roles of the shadow puppets from the Javanese wayang kulit.

MUSIC
To accompany traditional theater, dance, and other events, Indonesia's cultures have created many different kinds of

music. The best-known traditional music is the *gamelan*—a form of orchestral music from central and eastern Java and Bali that features various percussion instruments (mostly drums and gongs), flute, and xylophone. In Java, the gamelan also usually includes a melodic, bowed-stringed instrument, called the *rebab*, and sometimes background singing performed by both soloists and choruses. Traditionally, the gamelan is considered sacred by Indonesians, and the music and instruments are treated with great respect. Musicians take off their shoes while playing in the orchestra and audience members often offer gifts of incense and flowers.

In the past, the gamelan was played only during special occasions, such as ritual ceremonies, certain community celebrations, and for the royal family. Shadow puppet shows, too, have always been accompanied by a gamelan orchestra. Today, gamelan music is still used for puppet shows and ceremonies, but it is also performed for private social and cultural gatherings. Gamelan groups accompany many types of modern dances and theater, for example, and are even paid to play at private parties. Indeed, the music remains highly popular and provides a livelihood for many professional musicians in Indonesia.

Another type of traditional Indonesian music is *angklung*, which is performed using a traditional Sundanese bamboo musical instrument from West Java. The instrument, also called angklung, is a type of rattle made from several bamboo pipes that are placed in a frame. When this frame is shaken, the pipes slide and strike a bamboo or wooden rim, producing various melodic sounds. The angklung is usually played in groups of four or more people, but sometimes these assemblies can include as many as one hundred or more players. The angklung is often played for folk dances, rituals, or ceremonial events. For example, one traditional occasion for angklung music is at the end of the rice harvest, when the instrument is played to accompany workers as they head back to their village. Today, the instrument is widely used in West Java by local music groups that play at various festive events.

One of the most frequently heard modern styles of music in Indonesia is the *dangdut*, a style that originated in Indian pop music. Dangdut features wailing vocals, Islam-influenced lyrics, and a strong dance beat. As an Indonesian cultural Web site explains, "You'll hear dangdut everywhere, in food stalls, kiosks, markets."[19] In fact, dangdut is such a favorite that politicians schedule dangdut performances for their political rallies to increase the size of their audience.

Indonesians also love Western music. Both Michael Jackson and the Rolling Stones, for example, have performed before packed crowds in Indonesia. In addition, a number of Indonesian artists and bands play various types of Western music, including pop, rock, jazz, hip-hop, ska, and rap.

LITERATURE

Literature, too, has a long tradition in Indonesia. Although many of Indonesia's ethnic groups have not produced significant written literature, the majority populations in Java and Sumatra have been writing since before the arrival of the Dutch. Poetry, in particular, has been important to Indonesian culture. One form of traditional Indonesian poetry is called *Pantun*, a form of verse that consists of four lines, in which the second and fourth lines rhyme. Indonesia's most famous and greatest poet, however, is the late Chairil Anwar, an activist in the Indonesian independence movement in the 1940s. He is known for his idealistic and passionate poetry, which transformed Indonesian verse from its traditional forms. One of his most famous poems, called "Aku," was written in 1943 and contains the following stirring lines:

Though bullets should pierce my skin

I shall still strike and march forth

Wounds and poison shall I take . . .

'Til the pain and pang should disappear

And I should care even less

I want to live for another thousand years.[20]

Indonesian fiction is also highly developed among the country's dominant cultures. The most well-known modern Indonesian author is undoubtedly Pramoedya Ananta Toer, a Javanese novelist who, for his political views and criticism of the government, spent over fourteen years in jail during Soeharto's rule. His most famous work is a quartet of historical realist novels, called the *Buru Quartet*, about Indonesia

COCONUT PALMS

Coconut palms are often called the "Tree of Life" in Indonesia because they are one of its most important plants. The plant provides not only food, but also drinks, tools, shelter, and medicines. The fresh meat and milk of the coconut, for example, is found in hundreds of Indonesian dishes. Grated fresh coconut is used in many dishes. Sometimes meats are cooked in coconut milk. Coconut cream is used in desserts and forms the basis for many rich, thick sauces. Other dishes are made from the tender heart of the coconut palm. The meat, when dried, can be made into coconut oil that, in turn, is used in cooking oil, margarine, soap, candles, and perfume. In addition, the sap from the palm's flower buds is reduced to make palm sugar, which can be further processed to make alcoholic drinks as well as vinegars. Even the roots and coconut shells of the palm are important. The roots are useful as a gargle for sore throats and as a medicine for diarrhea. Coconut shells are made into ladles, and their husks are used for mattress stuffing and made into string.

Known as the "Tree of Life," the Indonesian coconut palm yields food, drink, oil, and medicines.

during the colonial era. The novels follow the life of Minke, a Javanese man who cannot reconcile his traditional Javanese beliefs with the Dutch colonial world, and therefore becomes involved in the Indonesian anticolonial movement.

Another legendary modern writer from Indonesia is Mochtar Lubis, known for exposing government corruption and inefficiency. He wrote *Twilight in Djakarta*, a novel set in the 1950s that attacked corruption in Jakarta and was banned by the government. Lubis was also jailed twice by both Soekarno and Soeharto, and his newspaper, the daily *Indonesia Raya*, was frequently banned by the Indonesian government. While in prison, he explained his philosophy on writing: "I am a stubborn old fool and am fully convinced that our era is the era of human freedom and human cooperation and not the era of human enslavement and inevitable confrontation. . . . But only a truly free press can help build up traditions of freedom . . . [and] fight against the abuse of power, against corruption—moral and material."[21] Today, Lubis remains a powerful symbol of courageous and independent journalism in Indonesia.

TRADITIONAL CRAFTS

Throughout all of Indonesia's cultures, however, the main form of artistic expression is traditional crafts. The tourist trade, by bringing larger markets, has boosted the craft industry throughout the country and led to high levels of craftsmanship. The most widely produced handicraft

A craftsman chisels away at an enormous wood carving. Indonesian wood carvings and other handicrafts are renowned throughout the world.

throughout the archipelago is Indonesia's intricate and sophisticated wood carvings. Statues, doors, religious objects, and furniture are the most commonly carved items, but many utilitarian items, such as bowls and baby carriers, are also hand carved. In Java and Bali, skilled artisans also produce special masks used primarily for the traditional dances of those areas.

Bali, in particular, produces some of the most intricate and beautiful wood carvings in all of Indonesia. Its crafters elaborately decorate their carvings with Hindu gods, demons, and fertility symbols. These have become highly popular among Western tourists, and in recent years wood carving has become a booming industry in Bali. Indonesian wood-carvers from southwest Irian Jaya are also famous for their work. They are known for their unique ancestor poles, called *mbis*, which are carved to depict dead ancestors and decorated with wings at the top of the pole to represent power. Traditionally, the poles were carved to accompany feasts celebrating successful head-hunting raids on enemy villages.

Textiles, too, are an important Indonesian craft. Perhaps the most well-known Indonesian textile is batik, a dyed fabric that displays intricate patterns. The patterns are produced by applying dye-resistant wax to the cloth so that decorative shapes and patterns emerge when the fabric is dyed. This process may be repeated several times as the fabric is dyed in various colors, often creating highly complex designs. Java is the home of Indonesian batik, and although once associated with Java's royal classes, batik today has grown into an important Javan industry that produces both traditional and modern designs.

Another type of Indonesian textile is ikat, an intricately patterned cloth made of threads that are carefully tie-dyed before they are woven together. Although ikat is made throughout the Indonesian archipelago, the center of production is on the islands of Nusa Tenggara. Here, many people still wear clothing made from this textile, displaying its many bright colors and intricate patterns. The third type of textile native to Indonesia is *songket*, an Islamic cloth in which gold or silver threads are woven with silk. It is commonly produced on Sumatra, where the Islamic religion is the strongest.

There are many other indigenous handicrafts throughout the islands. Bali, for example, has become identified
with its paintings. Traditionally, the paintings were used
only for temple decoration, but the arrival of westerners in
Bali following World War II inspired an explosion of this art
form. Today, Bali artists paint not only traditional Hindu-
influenced scenes, but also vividly colored scenes from
everyday life. Another sought-after Bali handicraft is gold
and silver jewelry, which is typically handwrought in both
traditional and modern designs. The nearby island of Lombok, meanwhile, is a center for both primitive ceramics as
well as finely woven baskets, some of which are decorated
with shells and beads.

Javanese artists, on the other hand, are known primarily
for the leather and wooden puppets used in the area's puppet shows. Javanese metal workers, however, are also
renowned for crafting intricate metal objects, such as bronze
daggers called kris. The carrying of the kris is an important
tradition among Javan men; even today, it is part of men's
formal dress and a symbol of masculinity. As travel writer
Turner explains, "The kris is no ordinary knife. It is said to be
endowed with supernatural powers; *adat* (traditional law)
requires that every father furnish his son with a kris upon his
reaching manhood, preferably an heirloom kris enabling his
son to draw on the powers of his ancestors which are stored
in the sacred weapon."[22]

FOOD

Indonesia's cultural diversity has also produced several unique
types of cuisine with many different influences. As food writer
Gwenda L. Hyman states, "Indonesian food is as diverse and
exciting as the people who live on this 3,200 mile long archipelago."[23] Indonesian food, for example, features items as disparate as fried rice with vegetables from China, curries from
India, and sweets and cakes common in Dutch fare.

Indonesia's cuisine, however, also includes many native
contributions, such as exotic tropical fruits, recently picked
vegetables, and delicious fresh fish and seafood. Another
widely used local ingredient is the coconut. Coconuts are
eaten directly from the shell, coconut milk is included in many
different dishes, and coconut cream is dolloped on top of
desserts. Many of Indonesia's famous spices also find their

A bride and groom in Banda Aceh sit with their wedding guests around a table heaped with a wide array of traditional foods.

way into Indonesian dishes. Surprisingly, however, one of these species—cloves—is no longer a part of Indonesian cooking. Instead, cloves are used in Indonesia mainly for flavoring tobacco, to make highly aromatic *krekek* (clove) cigarettes that can be smelled almost everywhere in Indonesia.

Nearly every island or region in Indonesia has its own style of cooking. Java, for example, specializes in a sophisticated blending of sweet and sour, and also some hot flavors that are used to cook a wide variety of fish and shellfish. Javans have a traditional feast, called *Slametan*, in which a large cone of rice is placed as the centerpiece, decorated with flowers, fruits, and vegetables, and surrounded by many different dishes with a mixture of textures and flavors. Some dishes will likely be crispy, such as deep-fried shrimp balls or anchovy fritters, others soupy noodle dishes or soft creamy coconut milk creations, and still others sweet and sour concoctions.

Bali, true to the character of its people, produces hot and spicy food flavored with chilies, garlic, and a spice called tumeric. Often chicken or duck is coated with a paste of these ingredients, wrapped in a banana leaf, and then barbecued

THREATS TO INDONESIA'S FREE PRESS

Throughout the Soekarno and Soeharto eras, Indonesia's media was subjected to restrictions that banned printing or saying anything that criticized the government. After Soeharto's ouster in 1998, however, Indonesia suddenly had broad freedom of the press. During the next few years, dozens of publications sprouted up and books, once forbidden, became easily available. In 1999, the government passed a new Press Law to guarantee press freedom. Yet in 2001, during President Megawati's administration, there were new government attempts to curb the press. Government interference with the press was most clearly seen in the government's control of information about events in Aceh, where rebels are fighting with government troops for independence from Indonesia. Journalists have been banned from the area, and the local Indonesian press has been under strong government pressure to avoid criticism of the government's actions or reporting about alleged human rights abuses there. Despite these problems, the Indonesian press today has much more freedom than ever before, and consequently, some observers conclude that these problems are just growing pains in the country's new democracy.

Government attempts to control the press became obvious during the administration of Indonesian president Megawati.

over a slow fire. The Balinese, unlike many people in other areas of Indonesia, also love pork. Eating pork is permitted by the Balinese Hindu religion but not by Islam. In fact, a famous Bali specialty is roast suckling pig, stuffed with spices and herbs and roasted on a spit until the skin is brown and crisp and the meat tender and succulent. Rice, fresh vegetables, grains, and seafood round out the typical Bali menu.

By comparison, other areas of Indonesia offer strikingly different diets. Irian Jaya and the Molluca Islands, for example, have no lowlands to grow rice, so the main foods there are flour made from the sago palm tree, the starchy root of the cassava plant, and sometimes plantains, a fruit similar to bananas. The flavors tend to be somewhat bland, mostly sweet and sour with an abundant use of local herbs.

TELEVISION, RADIO, NEWSPAPERS, AND MOVIES

In addition to its traditional arts, crafts, and foods, which reflect ancient and colonial experiences, Indonesia also is beginning to absorb many contemporary influences. Modern forms of entertainment, for example, such as television, radio, and cinema, are highly popular, although they have recently stirred a debate about values and foreign cultural influences.

All forms of media were restricted during the era of Soekarno's and Soeharto's rule; the government mainly used television programming to promote national unity and stability. Beginning in the early 1990s, however, the Soeharto government began to loosen its control over the flow of information, and this trend toward tolerating freedom of expression has mushroomed since Soeharto's ousting in 1998. Since that time, Indonesia has seen an increase of press publications from about three hundred to almost seven hundred, an increase of radio stations from about eight hundred to more than twelve hundred, and a growth of the number of television stations to about a dozen.

In 1990, for example, Soeharto deregulated television broadcasting in Indonesia. Quickly following this decree, several national commercial channels were established in Indonesia. The deregulation and privatization of television, in turn, created a debate about the content of this new form of culture. The lack of regulation allowed the broadcast of violent and sexually explicit foreign shows and films, which many Indonesians found objectionable for their children and incompatible with traditional Indonesian values. On the other hand, some Indonesians worried that allowing the government again to regulate television content would limit press freedoms and return the country to its authoritarian past. The result of this debate was a new broadcasting law that sets up a national communications commission to issue and monitor broadcasting licenses. In 2004, Indonesian courts upheld the new law as constitutional, allowing it to be implemented. Indonesian television, therefore, is now free of the strict government repression that characterized its recent past, but it will likely still be subject to some restrictions designed to make it responsive to the values of the Indonesian people.

Radio and newspapers are in much the same situation as Indonesian television since the fall of Soeharto. Freed from the years of government control under Soeharto, Indonesia exploded with new radio programs. As *Asian Times* reporter Kalinga Seneviratne notes, "Hundreds of community-owned radio stations [are] beaming local music and people's voices across the huge Indonesian archipelago today."[24] These radio broadcasters are, however, subject to the 2004 broadcasting law.

Newspapers, too, have relished new press freedoms. In 1999, the government passed a new law that explicitly protects freedom of the press. The new law, however, also contains restrictions—one requiring publishers to guarantee the right of the public to reply to the publisher's views, and another requiring publishers to respect religious norms, public morality, and the presumption of innocence. Like other forms of media, therefore, publishers of written materials still face some regulation.

SPORTS AND RECREATION

Besides pursuing traditional arts and activities, feasting on delicious foods, and enjoying modern forms of media, the most popular Indonesian pastime is sports. In fact, the Indonesian government has long encouraged Indonesians to participate in sports as a way to promote national unity. Throughout its history, the country has held an annual National Sports Day on September 9. On this day, athletes from across the country participate in various types and levels of sporting events.

Indonesians are especially fond of several organized, competitive sports. One unique sport is *sepak takraw*, a game in which two teams try to keep a rattan ball in the air with their feet. Another sport popular with both men and women is *pencak silat*, a martial art similar to karate. Badminton and

INDONESIA'S RELIGIOUS ARCHITECTURE

Indonesia is the site of some of the most ancient and magnificent examples of religious architecture. Borobudur Temple, for example, is one of the greatest Buddhist monuments in the world. Built in Central Java between A.D. 750 and 842, this colossal structure has ten floors, stands more than 113 feet (34.44m) high, and has dimensions of about 400 feet by 400 feet (121.92m by 121.92m). Java is also home to an even larger Hindu temple called Prambanan. With three giant temples that rise like giant spires more than 100 feet (30.48m) into the sky, 221 other smaller temples, and intricate sculpted details throughout, Prambanan Temple is easily one of the most majestic and beautiful temples in Southeast Asia. Bali, however, is home to more than 11,000 Hindu temples. Bali's most famous temple is the Temple of Pura Besakih, located on the slopes of Mt. Agung. The temple has three striking shrines similar in shape to Chinese pagodas, each constructed of many thatched tiers. Finally, the great Baiturrahman Mosque, built in 1883 in Aceh, is a fine example of Indonesian Islamic architecture. It has five onion-shaped domes, smooth white walls, and numerous pillars with beautiful ornamentation.

A view of the main entrance to the Hindu temple complex of Prambanan in central Java reveals the splendor of Indonesia's religious architecture.

tennis, too, are favorite sports, and Indonesians are strong players in professional-level badminton and tennis competitions. In fact, Rudy Hartono is a legendary badminton player from Indonesia who won the "All-England" Informal World Championship seven years in a row (1968 to 1974). Professional-level soccer and boxing are also quite popular, and running competitions have recently taken hold. Various regions even have their own indigenous sporting activities. Balinese men, for example, engage in cockfighting, or bird-fights, while the Madurese attend bullfights after each harvest season.

Indonesia's diversity clearly has resulted in a land of rich culture, delectable cuisine, and multiple diversions. The country's new democratic freedoms have, so far, only added to its cultural treasures. Whether these freedoms will continue to expand Indonesia's culture will be determined in the future as the nation struggles with its many social and political challenges.

CHALLENGES AHEAD

Political observers agree that Indonesia has made great progress over the last decade. Since the 1997 economic crisis, it has removed an authoritarian government and replaced it with a fledgling democracy, improved its economic condition significantly, made progress in fighting poverty, and sought to unite all Indonesians as one country. Yet the country today still faces daunting challenges on many fronts—economic, social, environmental, and political. The devastation of the recent tsunami only adds to the enormous hurdles already lying ahead for Indonesia's leaders and people.

RECOVERING FROM THE TSUNAMI

One of the most immediate and difficult challenges for Indonesia will be recovering from the tsunami that struck the islands on December 26, 2004. The towering waves from this natural disaster caused damage throughout the region, but the tsunami hit Indonesia the hardest, particularly the northern island of Sumatra. The grim death toll in Indonesia, according to government estimates announced in February 2005, is 243,530 Indonesians either dead or missing. Of this number, only about 111,171 have been confirmed to be dead and buried; the rest have simply gone missing since the tsunami. As a CNN report explains, "Compiling accurate figures for those killed or missing from the tsunami is almost impossible as many people were swept away by the waves into sea, while others were buried under rubble and mud."[25] Many of the dead were young children who could not run fast enough to escape the rising waters. As reporter Marianne Kearny explains, "The tsunami wiped out a generation of children . . . because the waves moved too fast to save them."[26] However, many children also survived only to lose parents and brothers and sisters. Early estimates suggested these tsunami orphans may number as many as thirty-five thousand.

Beyond the almost unfathomable loss of life, an additional one hundred thousand-plus Indonesians were injured in the disaster, and another six hundred thousand were left homeless when houses and businesses were destroyed. Most of these survivors now live in tents set up in temporary camps, where the new dangers are diseases created by unsanitary conditions. Many Indonesians also lost their future livelihoods. The UN has estimated, for example, that about ninety-six thousand acres of rice paddies were wiped out

Workers at the port of Jakarta load supplies of drinking water bound for survivors of the 2004 tsunami onto a ship.

along with as much as 70 percent of the country's already small fishing industry. Many of those affected were among the poorest of Indonesians. Altogether, according to Asian Development Bank estimates, as many as a million Indonesians may become completely destitute due to the tsunami.

Along with destroying lives, the tsunami wiped out whole villages, erased roads and communication systems, and severely damaged Indonesia's coastal environment. The powerful waves simply crushed buildings and other human construction in their path and either carried debris away or deposited it in huge piles on the beaches. Critical natural ecosystems and habitats, such as mangrove swamps, coral reefs, and sea grass beds, were also destroyed, and salty seawater polluted miles of river mouths and numerous underground wells. A preliminary estimate by the Indonesian government set the environmental damage alone at $675 million. In addition, experts say that a minimum of $4.5 billion will be needed to rebuild and replace destroyed buildings and infrastructure.

Yet in the wake of this horrible devastation, there was some good news. The Indonesian government, under the leadership of President Yudhoyono, quickly put together a relief and recovery strategy that mobilized financial and human resources to help the tsunami victims. After a slow start, emergency food and medical aid began reaching some of Indonesia's hardest hit areas in Aceh and other parts of Sumatra. The efforts prevented what could have been a second round of deaths from hunger and disease. As one of Indonesia's investors, Ray Jovanovich, explains, "The tsunami was Yudhoyono's first big test. . . . He has shown leadership, poise, and grace under extreme pressure."[27] Furthermore, because the disaster affected thousands of tourists and was seen around the world, the international community responded generously to pledge humanitarian and financial assistance. A total of more than $5 billion had been pledged as of February 2005, and in addition, major lending nations offered a temporary moratorium on Indonesia's international debt repayments. Despite these positives, however, as a January 2005 World Bank report states, "The nation is still struggling to come to terms with the enormity of the tragedy, the massive challenge of rebuilding lives and livelihoods, and the longer term task of healing the psychological wounds."[28]

GROWING THE ECONOMY

Another important question for Indonesia will be the effect the tsunami will have on the country's economy. Before the disaster, the economy was just finally regaining stability after being bankrupted by the 1997 monetary crisis. The Megawati administration, in particular, made significant progress by implementing reforms that gained the trust of the two major international financial institutions—the International Monetary Fund and the World Bank. During 2004, economic growth rebounded to around 5 percent, the highest growth since 1997. Exports increased; inflation stabilized; and consumer demand for products was strong.

Experts say the costs of tsunami recovery will be substantial and will likely cause economic growth to slow somewhat during 2005 and later years, especially in hardest-hit areas such as Aceh. Yet Indonesia's recent economic progress, analysts say, has positioned the country to be able to absorb much of the economic shock of the tragedy. The oil and gas industry, which makes up more than a third of Indonesia's economy, was luckily not affected. Also, the millions of reconstruction dollars that will be pumped into Indonesia are expected to offset some of the other economic losses. Some economists even predict that Indonesia's economy may flourish in 2005, producing growth even greater than in 2004.

Despite these rosy predictions, however, Indonesia's economy still has inherent weaknesses. These include a large foreign debt and problems such as recent acts of terrorism, unequal wealth distribution, government corruption, inadequate legal remedies in contract disputes, and banking system problems. All of these weaknesses, observers say, create an unfriendly climate for foreign investment. Experts say the keys to future growth, therefore, include continued debt reduction, anticorruption measures, additional internal market reforms, solutions to long-term social problems, and other actions designed to build the confidence of international and local investors. As economist Fauzi Ichsan explains, "If the [Indonesian] government can tackle problems that have deterred investment, the economy will continue to improve and optimism will last."[29] Indonesia's president, Yudhoyono, has pledged to follow this advice, and Indonesians are optimistic that he will succeed.

INDONESIA'S ECONOMY

Indonesia's economy is market-based, but the government still plays a significant role. There are more than 164 state-owned enterprises, and the government also sets prices on basic goods, such as fuel, rice, and electricity. The Indonesian economy grew at the rate of almost 7 percent from 1987 to 1997. These gains were reversed, however, by the 1997 Asian financial crisis, and today Indonesia's economy is just recovering to pre-1997 levels. The recovery was financed with international loans and aided by reforms recommended by the International Monetary Fund (IMF), an international institution that provides aid to developing countries. With its economy expanding, Indonesia withdrew from its IMF program at the end of 2003. Still, the number of unemployed and underemployed is estimated at 40 million and economic growth is only around 5 percent, less than is needed to put Indonesians back to work. More than a third of the economy is now based on production of oil and gas, but new reserves must be found to avoid depletion of these resources. However, the country is also a major producer of textiles and clothing, a popular site for tourism, and an exporter of plywood, chemical fertilizers, and agricultural products.

REDUCING POVERTY

A closely related economic problem is creating prosperity and eliminating poverty among Indonesia's battered population. The government, during President Soeharto's rule, made substantial progress on this front, and by the late 1990s had reduced the poverty to about 11 percent of the population. The 1997 crisis, however, reversed these gains, causing millions to lose their jobs, raising prices, and reducing almost half of the population to a life of poverty and starvation. Fortunately, Indonesia's economic reforms and growth since the 1997 crisis have helped Indonesia largely to repair much of the job loss, inflation, and poverty of the late 1990s. In 2004, experts calculated that the poverty rate was down to about 16.6 percent, relatively close to pre-1997 levels.

Despite the improvements, 16 percent of the population is a large number, and it does not reflect the many additional Indonesians who struggle to survive just above the meager poverty line that equates to earning one or two dollars per day. A large number of Indonesians therefore continue to live in deep or near poverty, and the recent tsunami has made this struggle for some even more difficult. The plight of the

Although Indonesia has made gains in reducing poverty, many living in remote areas such as this one continue to live in abysmal conditions.

poor is exacerbated by a lack of education and skills and limited access to health care. Although Indonesia, for low fees, provides six years of primary education and six years of high school, many poor children never make it to the secondary level, and few graduate from high school. Fewer still make it to college, which is prohibitively expensive for most Indonesians. Health care, too, is a problem. Although Indonesia has a national health-care system, many in rural areas still lack access to proper care.

Experts say several strategies will be important to reverse these conditions. Because many of the poorest Indonesians live in remote rural areas, where jobs are scarce and rice cultivation or other forms of agriculture are the economic mainstays, it will be important for Indonesia to invest in agriculture in these rural areas to boost production and improve farmers' incomes. Other strategies, the experts say, include programs to promote job creation, maintain household incomes through labor-intensive public works or other projects, and provide access to quality education and health services. Indonesia has formulated a formal poverty reduction strategy that includes many of these elements, and President Yudhoyono, soon after he was elected in 2004, signaled agreement with this plan. He promised to boost economic productivity, create jobs, and generously fund education and health-care programs. Foreign aid will help to pay for many of these programs, but positive economic advances will be the biggest determinant of whether the government will be able to afford these poverty reduction programs.

ENVIRONMENTAL CRISES

Another challenge for Indonesia's economy will be responding to environmental threats. Experts say the country's natural environment, although still magnificent, is deteriorating on all fronts. Illegal logging of Indonesia's forests is one of the most pressing issues. The depletion of forests, in turn, leads to other environmental problems, such as water pollution and water shortages. When forests are removed, the barren land can no longer catch rainfall, which normally would be cleansed as it sinks into the soil and is stored in underground wells. Instead, the water runs off, picks up pollutants, and often ends up polluting coastlines and threatening marine environments. The result is a shortage of clean water. For example, the country's highly populated islands, such as Java and Bali, no longer have enough water resources to meet population demand. The country also faces increasing air pollution created by decades of rapid economic development, significant population expansion, and government neglect.

Ecological protesters hold a banner in front of logs cut for export. Illegal logging in Indonesia's forests is a serious environmental concern.

The main reason for these problems, experts suggest, is weak government regulation. Although a broad array of environmental legislation has been passed by Indonesia in recent decades, it has not been properly enforced, largely because the government has been more concerned with growing the country's economy. As Indonesian reporter Muninggar Sri Saraswati explains, "The nation's economic policies are often considered exploitative from the environmental perspective."[30] The government, for example, has of-

RENEWABLE ENERGY

Because Indonesia today gets most of its energy from fossil fuels, such as oil, gas, and coal, its industrial development during recent decades has caused carbon pollution to increase by a whopping 271 percent. Concerns about this environmental pollution are leading Indonesia to explore renewable energy sources. Today, geothermal, wind, water, and solar energy account for only about 3 percent of Indonesian energy consumption, but their future potential is great. The World Bank has contributed to several large-scale renewable energy projects in Indonesia, including a "Solar Home System" project designed to electrify remote areas of the country. Solar technology is an attractive option for Indonesia because the country's numerous and widespread islands make a comprehensive electric system difficult and expensive to construct. Indonesia also has significant hydroelectric (water) potential. So far, however, only a few hydropower facilities have been built in Java and Irian Jaya. Perhaps the most promising renewable energy source, however, is geothermal—energy obtained from harnessing the heat from Indonesia's abundant volcanic activity. Government contracts for seven out of eleven geothermal projects were suspended during the country's recent economic crisis, but Indonesia's leaders hope to generate funding for additional renewable energy projects in the future.

Hundreds of motorists in Jakarta sit in a traffic jam. Air pollution from burning fossil fuels is a growing problem in Indonesia.

ten given a higher priority to promoting logging companies (typically owned by ex-government officials and military officers) and attracting foreign investment than to protecting Indonesia's rain forests. Perhaps this is really not surprising, however, considering the high economic value of the nation's timber to the nation's struggling economy. Although oil has always been a major export, the country was hard hit by the 1986 fall in world oil prices and, during the Soeharto years, came to depend upon timber as an important source of revenues. By 1990, as freelance writer Halesworth explains, "Indonesia [was producing] about 70 percent of the world's hardwood supply, earning it the nickname the 'Plywood King.'"[31] Today, Indonesia remains a large hardwood producer, but as much as 90 percent of its timber is produced illegally—either by companies with a legal permit who expand into adjacent protected forests, or by companies without permits. The government's failure to prevent these illegal activities is the leading cause of deforestation.

Since one of Indonesia's most valuable economic assets is its remarkable environment, advocates say actions must be taken soon to enforce environmental legislation. Otherwise, many ecosystems will be permanently lost and the costs of repairing environmental destruction in the future will far outweigh the short-term economic profits being reaped from environmental exploitation. Today, many are placing their hopes with Indonesia's president, Yudhoyono, who has promised to target four important environmental issues: safe drinking water and basic sanitation, renewable energy sources, illegal logging, and illegal fishing. Most observers agree that Yudhoyono's success or failure in improving the government's environmental record and creating more sustainable economic development will be critical to Indonesia's future.

RELIGIOUS UNREST AND SEPARATIST VIOLENCE

In addition to its many-faceted economic challenges, another of Indonesia's most persistent problems is its numerous social crises. Rising Islamic extremism is a chief concern since much of Indonesia's population is Muslim, yet ethnic separatist movements also threaten to tear the country apart.

In response to Islamic terrorist attacks, such as the 2002 Bali bombing, the Indonesian government tried and sentenced members of Jemaah Islamiyah, the Islamic extremist group found to have carried out the attacks. The government also passed antiterrorism legislation and, in October 2002, announced an eight-step program to combat terrorism that included measures to increase border security and to protect key economic infrastructure. Some observers criticize the government's response as weak, however. They note that although Abu Bakar Bashir, the mastermind behind Jemaah Islamiyah, was convicted of treason and other charges, he received only a thirty-month sentence for conspiracy because his treason conviction was reversed by the Indonesian Supreme Court. He will therefore be released, despite the fact that he has vowed to continue his fight against targets he views as enemies of Islam. Meanwhile, terrorist attacks in Indonesia have continued. A bombing at a hotel in Jakarta in 2003 killed twelve, while the attack in 2004 killed eleven people outside the Australian embassy.

Islamic extremists are also responsible for other rising religious violence in Indonesia. The eastern Indonesian islands of Maluki and Sulawesi, for example, have been plagued by increasing fighting between Muslims and Christians. In April 2002, masked gunmen massacred fourteen Christian villagers, and numerous Christian churches over the years have been attacked, bombed, or otherwise closed due to Muslim violence and pressure. This ongoing Muslim-Christian conflict so far has left more than ten thousand dead and displaced up to half a million refugees. Today, even moderate Muslims are being threatened by extremists who believe it is their god-given duty to establish an Islamic state throughout Southeast Asia. In Indonesia, extremists already have sought to amend the constitution to adopt Islamic law, or sharia, and have pushed for various legislative changes to make Indonesia more strictly Islamic. These efforts to date have largely failed, but in the absence of moderate Muslim leadership, politicians in Indonesia are facing increasing pressure to support extremist views.

In addition to religious conflicts, Indonesia still faces separatist violence. One region has already been lost to Indonesian separatists, when East Timor was granted its independence in 2002. In two other areas of the country—Irian Jaya and Aceh—guerrilla wars are still underway trying to gain independence from Indonesia. In Irian Jaya, fighting between government troops and rebels from the Free Papua

Movement has been a constant threat since the 1960s, with numerous civilian casualties. The rebels believe the government annexed the region unjustly. The dispute has continued despite legislation enacted by the Indonesian legislature in 2001 granting the area more resources and a greater degree of self-governance.

In Aceh, the violence has been equally as intense, and has afflicted the area since 1976, when the Free Aceh movement

TERRORIST GROUPS IN INDONESIA

Besides Jemaah Islamiyah, the group shown to be responsible for the 2002 bombings in Bali, Indonesia is home to several other radical Islamic groups, including Laskar Jihad, Laskar Jundullah, and Front Pembele Islam (the Islamic Defenders Front). Jemaah Islamiyah, the most prominent group, is believed to be a Southeast Asian branch of al Qaeda, the terrorist group that staged the 2001 attack on the World Trade Center in the United States. The group's spiritual leader is Abu Bakar Bashir, and its goal is to establish a large Islamic state encompassing all Muslim regions of Southeast Asia. Bashir has close ties with four other men described as Indonesia's most dangerous terrorists: Hambali (alias Ridwan Isamuddin); Abdur Rahman al-Ghozi, Muhammad Iqbal bin Abdurrahman (alias Abu Jibril); and Agus Dwikarna. All of these men have been connected to terrorist bombings of Christian churches and other sites in recent years. Both Laskar Jihad and Laskar Jundullah are Islamic militia groups engaged in Muslim-Christian fighting, the former in the Maluka Islands and the latter in South Sulawesi. The Islamic Defenders Front, on the other hand, is involved primarily in staging Islamic demonstrations in Jakarta.

Armed with swords, members of the extremist Islamic group Laskar Jihad protest outside the Indonesian parliament in 1999.

On October 20, 2004, newly elected president Susilo Bambang Yudhoyono shares with the nation his plan to improve democracy in Indonesia.

was formed to create a separate Islamic state. Since talks between the two sides broke down in 2002, the struggle has escalated, and today rebels are believed to control as many as two-thirds of the villages in Aceh. Because the area is the site of rich oil and natural gas resources, however, observers say the Indonesian government is unlikely ever to give in to independence demands. Many hoped the recent tsunami, by focusing everyone on relief work instead of fighting, would provide an inroad to resolving tensions in Aceh. In fact, immediately following the tsunami, the two sides declared an informal cease-fire and truce talks began in Helsinki, Finland. Indonesia's President Yudhoyono also flew to Aceh and made promises to rebuild the area. However, violence erupted once again as the military renewed its hunt for suspected rebel fighters.

In the future, resolving those internal threats will be critical to Indonesia's security. Many experts believe that peaceful and negotiated solutions, in the end, will likely provide the most lasting solutions. President Yudhoyono, for his part, has made it clear that he wants to negotiate an end to the wars in Irian Jaya and to Aceh disputes by granting more regional autonomy and increasing economic prosperity in those regions. Yudhoyono's election has also raised hopes that, with his military background and experience as a former security minister involved in investigating the Bali attack, he will take strong actions against Islamic extremists. Indonesians, as well as others throughout the world, are waiting to see if these promises can be turned into results.

MAINTAINING INDONESIA'S DEMOCRACY

Amidst these various economic and social struggles, Indonesia is also trying to nurture and improve its young and still-fragile democracy. Observers agree that during the last several years Indonesia has already made impressive gains. It has created a relatively free press, separated the military from the legislature, and tried to decentralize the government to make it more effective given the country's multiple regions.

The highly successful 2004 elections gave many hope, as a large majority of Indonesians went to the polls to elect a democratic president and parliament. President Yudhoyono, in the early months of his term, has also created a favorable impression by speaking about the importance of democracy, accountability, rooting out corruption, and good governance. The reality of accomplishing these goals, however, is daunting. Yudhoyono first must put together a working coalition in Indonesia's parliament to have any hope of being effective. Even then, progress may be slow, because so many of Indonesia's problems are so entrenched.

Moreover, many observers say that Yudhoyono's success at governing will likely depend on whether he can rein in the Indonesian military, which has long had a reputation for corruption and human rights abuses. In the past, the army has resisted such reform efforts. For example, although Indonesia in recent years has formally placed the military under civilian control and restricted its role to national defense, Indonesia's military establishment has sought to maintain its historic authoritarian influence over the government, legislature, and judiciary. Many are watching to see what, exactly, Yudhoyono will be able to accomplish in this arena.

However, with the blessings of a growing economy and a newly empowered Indonesian public that desperately wants positive change, Indonesia's future looks much brighter than its past. As economist Anton Gunawan explains, "A wind of change and optimism is blowing [in Indonesia]."[32] How Indonesia's new president handles the many challenges that lie before him during the next few years will determine whether that optimism is justified.

Facts About Indonesia

Geography

Location: Southeastern Asia, archipelago between the Indian Ocean and the Pacific Ocean

Area: total: 741,096 square miles (1,926,899.6 sq. km); land: 705,189 square miles (1,833,491.4 sq. km); water: 35,907 square miles (93,358.2 sq. km)

Area comparative: Slightly less than three times the size of Texas

Border countries: East Timor, Malaysia, Papua New Guinea

Coastline: 33,924 miles (54,278.4km)

Climate: Tropical, hot, humid; more moderate in highlands

Terrain: Mostly coastal lowlands; larger islands have interior mountains

Natural resources: Petroleum, tin, natural gas, nickel, timber, bauxite, copper, fertile soils, coal, gold, silver

Land use: Arable land, 11.32 percent; permanent crops, 7.23 percent; other, 81.45 percent (2001 estimate)

Natural hazards: Occasional floods, severe droughts, tsunamis, earthquakes, volcanoes, forest fires

People

Population: 238,452,952 (July 2004 estimate)

Age structure: 0–14 years: 29.4 percent (male 35,635,790; female 34,416,854) 15–64 years: 65.5 percent (male 78,097,767; female 78,147,909) 65 years and over: 5.1 percent (male 5,308,986; female 6,845,646) (2004 estimate)

Birth rate: 21.11 births/1,000 population (2004 estimate)

Death rate: 6.26 deaths/1,000 population (2004 estimate)

Infant mortality rate: 36.82 deaths/1,000 live births (2004 estimate)

Life expectancy: Total population: 69.26 years; male: 66.84 years; female: 71.8 years (2004 estimate)

Fertility rate: 2.47 children born/woman (2004 estimate)

Ethnic groups: Javanese 45 percent, Sundanese 14 percent, Madurese 7.5 percent, coastal Malays 7.5 percent, other 26 percent

Religions: Muslim 88 percent, Protestant 5 percent, Roman Catholic 3 percent, Hindu 2 percent, Buddhist 1 percent, other 1 percent (1998 estimate)

Languages: Bahasa Indonesian (official, modified form of Malay), English, Dutch, local dialects (the most widely spoken of which is Javanese)

Literacy rate (age 15 and over): Total population, 87.9 percent; male, 92.5 percent; female: 83.4 percent (2002 estimate)

GOVERNMENT

Country name: Republic of Indonesia (short form: Indonesia)

Form of government: Republic

Capital: Jakarta

Administrative divisions: Thirty provinces, two special regions*, and one special capital city district**: Aceh*, Bali, Banten, Bengkulu, Gorontalo, Irian Jaya Barat, Jakarta Raya**, Jambi, Jawa Barat, Jawa Tengah, Jawa Timur, Kalimantan Barat, Kalimantan Selatan, Kalimantan Tengah, Kalimantan Timur, Kepulauan Bangka Belitung, Kepulauan Riau, Lampung, Maluku, Maluku Utara, Nusa Tenggara Barat, Nusa Tenggara Timur, Papua, Riau, Sulawesi Barat, Sulawesi Selatan, Sulawesi Tengah, Sulawesi Tenggara, Sulawesi Utara, Sumatera Barat, Sumatera Selatan, Sumatera Utara, Yogyakarta

National holiday: Independence Day, August 17, 1945

Date of independence: Independence proclaimed, August 17, 1945; independence recognized by the Netherlands, December 27, 1949

Constitution: August 1945, abrogated by Federal Constitution of 1949 and Provisional Constitution of 1950; restored July 5, 1959

Legal system: Based on Roman-Dutch law, substantially modified by indigenous concepts and by new criminal procedures and election codes

Suffrage: 17 years of age; universal and married persons regardless of age

Executive branch; Chief of state—President Susilo Bambang Yudhoyono (since October 20, 2004) and Vice President Muhammad Yusuf Kalla (since October 20, 2004) (Note: The president is both the chief of state and head of government.); cabinet—appointed by the president; elections—president and vice president elected by direct vote of the citizenry

Legislative branch: Unicameral House of Representatives (Dewan Perwakilan Rakyat or DPR)—550 seats; members serve five-year terms; House of Regional Representatives (Dewan Perwakilan Daerah or DPD)—constitutionally mandated role includes providing legislative input to DPR on issues affecting regions; People's Consultative Assembly (Majelis Permusyawaratan Rakyat or MPR)—consists of popularly elected members in DPR and DPD; has role in inaugurating and impeaching president and in amending constitution; MPR does not formulate national policy; elections—last held April 5, 2004 (next to be held in April 2009)

Judicial branch: Supreme Court (or Mahkamah Agung)—justices appointed by the president from a list of candidates approved by the legislature; a separate Constitutional Court (or Makhama Konstitusi) was created by the president on August 16, 2003

ECONOMY

Gross Domestic Product (GDP): $758.8 billion (2003 estimate); real
   growth, 4.1 percent (2003 estimate); GDP per capita, $3,200 (2003
   estimate); GDP composition, agriculture 16.6 percent, industry
   43.5 percent, services 39.9 percent (2003 estimate)

Labor force: 105.7 million (2003 estimate)

Population below poverty line: 27 percent (1999 estimate)

Unemployment rate: 8.7 percent (2003 estimate)

Industries: Petroleum and natural gas, textiles, apparel, footwear, min-
   ing, cement, chemical fertilizers, plywood, rubber, food, tourism

Agricultural products: Rice, cassava (tapioca), peanuts, rubber, cocoa,
   coffee, palm oil, copra, poultry, beef, pork, eggs

Exports: $63.89 billion (2003 estimate)

Imports: $40.22 billion (2003 estimate)

Debt: $235.7 billion (2003 estimate)

Currency: Indonesian rupiah (IDR)

NOTES

INTRODUCTION: A DANGEROUS PARADISE

1. Bill Dalton, *Bali Handbook*. Chico, CA: Moon, 1997, p. 1.

CHAPTER 1: A NATION OF ISLANDS

2. Peter Turner, Marie Cambon, Paul Greenway, Brendan Delahunty, and Emma Miller, *Indonesia*. Hawthorn, Victoria, Australia: Lonely Planet, 2000, p. 17.

3. Dan Murphy, "Indonesia Has Seen Its Share of Disasters," *USA Today*, December 29, 2004. www.usatoday.com/news/world/2004-12-29-indonesia-history_x.htm.

4. Peter Halesworth, "Indonesia Plundering Indonesia's Rain Forests," 1990. http://multinationalmonitor.org/hyper/issues/1990/10/mm1090_05.html.

CHAPTER 2: A DUTCH COLONY

5. Datus C. Smith Jr., *The Land and People of Indonesia*. New York: J.B. Lippincott, 1968, p. 35.

6. Robert Crib and Colin Brown, *Modern Indonesia: A History Since 1945*. Essex, England: Longman Group, 1995, p. 5.

7. Donald M. Seekins, "Historical Setting," *Indonesia: A Country Study*, William H. Frederick and Robert L. Worden, eds. Washington, DC: Federal Research Division, Library of Congress, 1992, p. 21.

8. Seekins, "Historical Setting," *Indonesia*, p. 40.

9. M.C. Ricklefs, *A History of Modern Indonesia Since C. 1300*. Stanford, CA: Stanford University Press, 1993, p. 217.

CHAPTER 3: THE ROAD TO DEMOCRACY

10. Seekins, "Historical Setting," *Indonesia*, p. 49.

11. Quoted in Turner, Cambon, Greenway, Delahunty, and Miller, *Indonesia*, p. 17.

12. Crib and Brown, *Modern Indonesia*, p. 102.

13. Quoted in Seekins, "Historical Setting," *Indonesia*, p. 61.

14. Turner, Cambon, Greenway, Delahunty, and Miller, *Indonesia*, p. 36.

CHAPTER 4: INDONESIAN SOCIETY

15. BBC, "Country Profile: Indonesia," 2004. http://news.bbc.co.uk/1/hi/world/asia-pacific/country_profiles/1260544.stm.

16. Turner, Cambon, Greenway, Delahunty, and Miller, *Indonesia*, p. 55.

17. Joshua Project, "Madura of Indonesia," February 3, 2004. www.joshuaproject.net/peopctry.php?rop3=105999&rog3=ID.

18. Dalton, *Bali Handbook*, p. 50.

CHAPTER 5: A MIX OF CULTURES

19. Budi Rahardjo, "Indonesian Music," Indonesian homepage, December 2004. http://indonesia.insan.web.id/music.

20. Quoted in Pegasos, "Anwar Chairil (1922–1949)," 2000. www.kirjasto.sci.fi/chairil.htm.

21. Quoted in Horas Mandailing, "Mochtar Lubis," July 6, 2003. www.mandailing.org/mandailinge/mlubis.html.

22. Turner, Cambon, Greenway, Delahunty, and Miller, *Indonesia*, p. 79.

23. Gwenda L. Hyman, *Cuisines of Southeast Asia*. New York: John Wiley & Sons, 1993, p. 133.

24. Kalinga Seneviratne, "Indonesia's Radio Revolution," *Asian Times Online*, July 11, 2003. www.atimes.com/atimes/Southeast_Asia/EG11Ae02.html.

Chapter 6: Challenges Ahead

25. CNN, "Tsunami Deaths Soar Past 212,000," January 19, 2005. www.cnn.com/2005/WORLD/asiapcf/01/19/asia.tsunami.

26. Marianne Kearny, "Tsunami Orphans," *U.S. News & World Report*, vol. 138, no. 3, January 24, 2005.

27. Quoted in Assif Shameen, "Indonesia: The Right Leader in a Time of Trial?," *Business Week*, January 24, 2004. http://yahoo.businessweek.com/magazine/content/05_04/b3917087.htm.

28. World Bank, "Indonesia: New Directions," The World Bank Brief for the Consultative Group of Indonesia, January 19–20, 2005. http://siteresources.worldbank.org/INTINDONESIA/Resources/Publication/2800161106130305439/CGI_Indonesia_New_Direction.pdf.

29. Quoted in Political Gateway, "2004 Review—Indonesia's Economic Future Bright but Caution Still Needed," December 20, 2004. www.politicalgateway.com/news/read.html?id=2238.

30. Muninggar Sri Saraswati, "Indonesia: The Country's Rich Natural Resources Endangered," *Jakarta Post*, December 28, 2004. http://forests.org/articles/reader.asp?linkid=37647.

31. Halesworth, "Indonesia Plundering Indonesia's Rain Forests," 1990. http://multinationalmonitor.org/hyper/issues/1990/10/mm1090_05.html.

32. Quoted in Shameen, "Indonesia: The Right Leader in a Time of Trial?," *Business Week*, January 24, 2004. http://yahoo.businessweek.com/magazine/content/05_04/b3917087.htm.

CHRONOLOGY

500,000 years ago
Java Man and his descendants live in small hunting and gathering groups in Indonesia.

3000 B.C.
Migrants, called "Malays," travel to the region from southern China and Indochina and eventually develop organized societies.

A.D. 600s–700s
Indian traders travel to Indonesia and two Hindu kingdoms are established: Srivijaya in eastern Sumatra and Mataram in Java. The Mataram people later become part of the Buddhist Sailendra kingdom.

A.D. 1000s
Arab traders begin spreading Islam throughout Indonesia.

A.D. 1200s
The last great Hindu kingdom, Majapahit, develops in Indonesia.

Late A.D. 1400s
Portuguese explorers travel to Indonesia.

A.D. 1500s
Indonesia is home to two Muslim kingdoms: the Melaka kingdom in Java and the Makassar kingdom in southwestern Saluwesi.

1596
The first Dutch expedition, led by Cornelius de Houtman, arrives in Indonesia, followed by traders from the Dutch East India Company.

1799
Indonesia becomes a Dutch colony called the Dutch East Indies.

1825–1830
The Java War erupts after a revolt led by Pangeran Diponegoro against Dutch rule over Java.

1928
The Partai Nasional Indonesia (PNI), a nationalist group led by Achmed Soekarno, is founded to fight against Dutch rule.

1942
Japan invades the Dutch East Indies during World War II.

1945
The Japanese help independence leader Soekarno prepare for Indonesia's independence, which Soekarno declares at war's end.

1949
The Dutch recognize Indonesian independence.

1949–1965
Soekarno rules Indonesia as an authoritarian president.

1965
A coup against Soekarno is foiled by the military, led by General Soeharto. In the aftermath, hundreds of thousands of suspected Communists are massacred.

1966
Sukarno hands over emergency powers to General Soeharto, who becomes president in 1967.

1969–1998
Soeharto rules Indonesia as an authoritarian president.

1997
An Asian financial crisis begins and destroys Indonesia's economy.

1998

Widespread protests and rioting lead to the fall of Soeharto. B.J. Habibie becomes president.

1999

Free elections are held in Indonesia, and Abdurrahman Wahid becomes president.

2000

Political scandals arise in Wahid's administration, resulting in mass political demonstrations.

2001

Wahid is replaced as president by Vice President Megawati Sukarnoputri.

2002

In April, East Timor becomes an independent nation. In October, a bomb explodes at a Bali nightclub, killing 202 people, most of them tourists.

2003

In July, legislators pass constitutional changes to allow Indonesian voters to elect directly their president and vice president. In August, a car bomb explodes outside a hotel in Jakarta, killing 14 people.

2004

On September 9, a bomb explodes outside the Australian embassy in Jakarta, killing 11 people. On September 20, Indonesia holds its first direct presidential elections, and Susilo Bambang Yudhoyono is elected president. On December 26, Indonesia is hit by a powerful tsunami, leaving as many as 243,530 people dead or missing.

FOR FURTHER READING

BOOKS

Frederick Fisher, *Indonesia*. Milwaukee, WI: Gareth Stevens, 2000. A young adult book that discusses the geography, history, government, commerce, people, and culture of Indonesia.

Kathy Furgang, *Krakatoa: History's Loudest Volcano*. New York: Powerkids, 2001. A young adult book about Indonesia's Krakatoa volcanic eruption.

Rita Golden Gelman, *Rice Is Life*. New York: Henry Holt, 2000. A children's book about the importance of rice to life on the island of Bali in the country of Indonesia.

Mirpuri Gouri, *Indonesia*. New York: Marshall Cavendish, 2002. A children's book that provides an overview of Indonesia's geography, history, government, economy, and environment.

Janet Riehecky, *Indonesia*. Mankato, MN: Bridgestone, 2002. This children's book introduces the geography, animals, food, and culture of Indonesia.

WEB SITES

Lonely Planet (www.lonelyplanet.com). A travel Web site that contains useful information about various aspects of life and travel in Indonesia, including discussions of the country's history, culture, and environment.

Nation by Nation (www.nationbynation.com). A commercial Web site that provides basic information about Indonesia's history, geography, economy, and government.

U.S. Central Intelligence Agency (CIA) (www.cia.gov/cia). This U.S. government Web site gives geographical, political, economic, and other information on Indonesia.

U.S. Department of State (http://travel.state.gov). A U.S. government Web site providing practical information and travel warnings for people who plan to visit Indonesia.

WORKS CONSULTED

BOOKS

Robert Crib and Colin Brown, *Modern Indonesia: A History Since 1945*. Essex, England: Longman Group, 1995. This book provides a scholarly history of Indonesia, covering the period from colonial times until the last years of President Soeharto's regime.

Bill Dalton, *Bali Handbook*. Chico, CA: Moon, 1997. This is a travel handbook and comprehensive guide to the island of Bali in the country of Indonesia.

William H. Frederick and Robert L. Worden, eds., *Indonesia: A Country Study*. Washington, DC: Federal Research Division, Library of Congress, 1992. This Library of Congress study and report on Indonesia provides a good overview of its history, society, economy, government, military, and foreign policy.

Gwenda L. Hyman, *Cuisines of Southeast Asia*. New York: John Wiley & Sons, 1993. This is an engaging book about various southeast Asian cuisines, including those of Indonesia.

M.C. Ricklefs, *A History of Modern Indonesia Since C. 1300*. Stanford, CA: Stanford University Press, 1993. This very scholarly treatise on Indonesia's history analyzes issues such as the effects of Islam, colonialism, and independence on the region.

Datus C. Smith, *The Land and People of Indonesia*. New York: J.B. Lippincott, 1968. This somewhat dated overview of Indonesia contains still-relevant information about the country's geography and history.

Ian Thornton, *Krakatau: The Destruction and the Reassembly of an Island Ecosystem*. Cambridge, MA: Harvard University Press, 1996. This is a case study of the Krakatoa disaster and its aftermath, written by a recognized expert on the subject.

101

Peter Turner, Marie Cambon, Paul Greenway, Brendan De-
    lahunty, and Emma Miller, *Indonesia*. Hawthorn, Victoria,
    Australia: Lonely Planet, 2000. This travel guide to In-
    donesia contains valuable discussions of the country's
    history, geography, climate, environment, government,
    economy, people, and cultures.

PERIODICALS/NEWSPAPERS

Australasian Business Intelligence, "Plunged into Poverty:
    Tsunami May Increase Poverty in Affected Countries," Jan-
    uary 13, 2005.

Andrew Burrell, "Bright Hopes as Horror Recedes," *Aus-
    tralasian Business Intelligence*, January 12, 2005.

Michael Elliott, "Sea of Sorrow: The World Suffers an Epic
    Tragedy as a Tsunami Spreads Death Across Asia," *Time*,
    January 10, 2005, vol. 165, no. 2.

Sukino Harisuarto, "Analysis: Megawati Fails to Cut Corrup-
    tion," *United Press International*, July 24, 2002.

Marianne Kearny, "Tsunami Orphans," *U.S. News & World
    Report*, January 24, 2005, vol. 138, no. 3.

Martin Sieff, "Analysis: Megawati Succeeds Against Odds,"
    United Press International, October 21, 2003.

Evan Thomas and George Wehrfritz, "Tide of Grief; The Earth
    Shrugged, and More than 140,000 Died," *Newsweek*, Janu-
    ary 10, 2005.

INTERNET SOURCES

Abigail Abrash, "Papua: Another East Timor?," *Foreign Policy
    in Focus*, vol. 5, no. 37, October 2000. www.fpif.org/briefs/
    vol5/v5n37papua.html.

Aceh Tourism, "Baiturrahman Mosque." www.acehtourism.
    com/BandaAceh.asp.

Kim Barker, "Moderate Islam Faces Challenge in Indonesia,"
    Chicago Tribune, December 15, 2004. www.chicago
    tribune.com/news/nationworld/chi-0412150290dec15,1,
    5988997.story?ctrack=1&cset=true.

Bali Advertising, "Bali Tradition and Religion: Bali's Caste System." www.baliadvertising.com/tradition/bali_caste.shtml.

BBC, "Country Profile: Indonesia," 2004. http://news.bbc.co.uk/1/hi/world/asia-pacific/country_profiles/1206544.stm.

BBC News, "Speech That Ended an Epoch," May 21, 1998. http://news.bbc.co.uk/1/hi/events/indonesia/latest_news/97884.stm.

Borbudur, Prambana & Ratu Boko Official Web Site, "Borobudur Temple" and "Prambanan Temple." www.borobudurpark.com/borobudur.php.

Building Human Security in Indonesia, "Background of the Conflict in Aceh," 2001. www.preventconflict.org/portal/main/maps_sumatra_background.php.

Consultative Group on Indonesia Meeting, "The Republic of Indonesia Experiences in Developing Poverty Reduction Strategy," World Bank, December 10, 2003. http://siteresources.worldbank.org/INTINDONESIA/Resources/CGI03/13th-CGI-Dec10-11-03/Djoharis.pdf.

CNN, "Tsunami Deaths Soar Past 212,000," January 19, 2005. www.cnn.com/2005/WORLD/asiapcf/01/19/asia.tsunami.

Energy Information Administration, U.S. Department of Energy, "Indonesia: Environmental Issues," February 2004. www.eia.doe.gov/emeu/cabs/indoe.html.

Famous Muslims, "Ahmed Sukarno," 2003. www.famousmuslims.com/Sukarno.htm.

Geography IQ, "Indonesia—Economy," 2002–2003. www.geographyiq.com/countries/id/Indonesia_economy_summary.htm.

Peter Halesworth, "Indonesia Plundering Indonesia's Rain Forests," 1990. http://multinationalmonitor.org/hyper/issues/1990/10/ mm1090_05.html.

Horas Mandailing, "Mochtar Lubis," July 6, 2003. www.mandailing.org/mandailinge/mlubis.html.

Human Rights Watch, "Indonesia: Media Under Attack in

Aceh," November 26, 2003. http://hrw.org/press/2003/11/aceh112603.htm.

Jakarta Post, "No More Living Dangerously: Environment at a Crossroads," December 30, 2004. www.illegallogging.info/news.php?newsId=621.

Joshua Project, "Madura of Indonesia," February 3, 2004. www.joshuaproject.net/peopctry.php?rop3=105999&rog3=ID.

Lonely Planet, "East Timor: History, 2004," http://www.lonelyplanet.com/destinations/south_east_asia/east_timor/history.htm.

Brenna Lorenz, "Komodo Dragons and Their Islands," *Heptune*, February 27, 2001. www.heptune.com/komodo.html.

Dan Murphy, "Indonesia Has Seen Its Share of Disasters," *USA Today*, December 29, 2004. www.usatoday.com/news/world/2004-12-29-indonesia-history_x.htm.

Pegasos, "Anwar Chairil (1922–1949)," 2000. www.kirijasto.sci.fi/chairil.htm.

Political Gateway, "2004 Preview—Indonesia's Economic Future Bright but Caution Still Needed," December 20, 2004. www.politicalgateway.com/news/read.html?id=2238.

Budi Rahardjo, "Indonesian Music," Indonesian homepage, December 2004. http://indonesia.insan.web.id/music.

Sacred Sites, "Sacred Sites of Bali," 2005. http://sacredsites.com/asia/bali/sacred_sites.html.

Muninggar Sri Saraswati, "Indonesia: The Country's Rich Natural Resources Endangered," *Jakarta Post*, December 28, 2004. http://forests.org/articles/reader.asp?linkid=376/47.

Kalinga Seneviratne, "Indonesia's Radio Revolution," *Asian Times Online*, July 11, 2003. www.atimes.com/atimes/Southeast_Asia/EG11Ae02.html.

Settlement, "Sports and Recreation." www.settlement.org/cp/english/indonesia/sports.html.

Assif Shameen, "Indonesia: The Right Leader in a Time of Trial?," *Business Week*, January 24, 2004. http://yahoo.businessweek.com/magazine/content/05_04/b3917087.htm.

Tiarma Siboro, "Skepticism of Military Reform," *Jakarta Post*, December 26, 2004. www.etan.org/et2004/december/26-31/30skept.htm.

Ahmed Soekarno, "Pidato-Soekarno ("Trikora") Speech," Papua Web, www.papuaweb.org/goi/pidato/1961-12-jo gyakarta.html.

Spice Islands home page, "The Spice Islands." www.iol.ie/~spice?Indones.htm.

Sunday Times, "Death Toll in Tsunami Disaster Tops 296,000," February 9, 2005. www.suntimes.co.za/zones/sundaytimes NEW/basket7st/basket7st1107927953.aspx.

UN News Centre, "Beyond Huge Tsunami Death Toll, Indonesia Faces Massive Loss of Livelihoods," January 25, 2005. www.un.org/apps/news/story.asp?NewsID=13128 &Cr=tsunami&Cr1=.

Martin van Bruinessen, "The Violent Fringe of Indonesia's Radical Islam," December 17, 2002. Berubah, www.berubah.org/BaliBombing/ISIM_1.htm.

Wikipedia, "Susilo Bambang Yudhoyono," January 18, 2005. http://en.wikipedia.org/wiki/Susilo_Bambang_Yudhoy ono.

World Bank, The World Bank Brief for the Consultative Group of Indonesia, "Indonesia: New Directions," January 19–20, 2005. http://siteresources.worldbank.org/INTINDONE SIA/Resources/Publication/280016 1106130305439/CGI_ Indonesia_New_Direction.pdf.

Anna Yeadell, "Indonesian Press under Pressure," Radio Netherlands, March 22, 2004. www2.rnw.nl/rnw/en/fea tures/development/040322agl.html.

H.E. Susilo Bambang Yudhoyono, President of Indonesia, Inauguration Speech at State Palace, Jakarta, October 20, 2004, US–ASEAN Business Council. www.us-asean.org/ Indonesia/sby_speech.asp.

INDEX

PICTURE CREDITS

ABOUT THE AUTHOR

Debra A. Miller is a writer and lawyer with a passion for current events and history. She began her law career in Washington, D.C., where she worked on legislative, policy, and legal matters in government, public interest, and private law firm positions. She now lives with her husband in Encinitas, California. She has written and edited publications for legal publishers, as well as numerous books and anthologies on historical and political topics.